Praise for *Home to You*:

"A story of love, family, and finding ourselves through the ups and downs of life all amidst the madness of Thanksgiving. You won't be disappointed!"

– Amazon reviewer

"Their romantic tension is strong and their emotional conflicts are believable and relatable."

– Amazon reviewer

"I stayed up late to finish 'Home to You' by Dana Nussio. I had to know how it ended before I went to sleep. This is a story many of us can relate to about love, family and the sacrifices we make for the love of someone else.

– GoodReads reviewer

Praise for **True Blue** series:

"Taut drama. Pure chemistry. Dana Nussio's characters always shine."

– NYT best-selling author Ruth Ryan Langan,
aka R.C. Ryan

"A satisfying emotion-layered beginning to a new MUST READ series."

– Best-selling author Nancy Gideon

Home to You

Dana Nussio

Published by DLN Publications, LLC

Cover art by Victoria Cooper Art
Edited by Laurie Kuna and Alexa Nussio

ISBN 978-1-7325198-0-0

Dedication

To my writer pals, Isabelle Drake, Loralee Lillibridge and Nancy Gideon, who each helped with this story in her own way, and to Laurie Kuna and Alexa Nussio, who helped to make it shine. Where would I be without all of you?

Dear Reader,

Fall is one of my favorite times of the year, and I love all holidays, so I had a wonderful time telling Lily and C.J.'s Thanksgiving story. I was also excited to have the chance to revisit the real-life small town of Brighton, Michigan, where my **True Blue** series is set. *HOME TO YOU* offers just a taste of the **True Blue** world in a story about the prodigal daughter of a late Michigan State Police sergeant and the love she left behind. For a heartier serving, check out my first Harlequin Romantic Suspense, *THE SINGLE MOM'S SECRETS*, to be released in February 2019.

   After the Harlequin Superromance line was canceled, I was happy for the chance to bring **True Blue** to its new home at Romantic Suspense. If you want to get to know the Brighton Post clan right now, look for these Superromance titles: *STRENGTH UNDER FIRE* and *FALLING FOR THE COP.*

   To learn more about these and all my books, written as Dana Nussio and as Dana Corbit, check out my website, www.dananussio.com. While you're there, sign up for my newsletter, so you can stay up-to-date on the latest fun news. I love staying in contact with readers. Connect with me through my Dana Nussio Facebook author page and Twitter @DanaNussio1 or send me a note at P.O. Box 5, Novi, MI 48376-0005.

Happy reading!
Dana Nussio

Chapter 1

T Minus 66 Hours and 30 Minutes until Thanksgiving Dinner

THE ROTATING METAL of the baggage carousel chugged along an endless circuit at Detroit Metro Airport, the thin plates consuming and then regurgitating themselves at the next turn. The same four suitcases, all black, made the trip three times, like abandoned wooden horses on a silent merry-go-round.

Lily Monroe straightened her shoulders to hold her place in the line of holiday travelers wedged around the carousel's perimeter. They leaned forward as one body to view any new bags birthed through the hole at the circuit's center.

Great. As if returning home to Brighton wouldn't be hard enough, now the airline had probably lost her luggage. Lily squeezed her eyes shut to head off the tears that threatened. When she opened them again, more suitcases had surfaced.

She crossed her arms and widened her stance. She'd already made the two-thousand-mile trip from Los Angeles. She could do the rest. Just five days with Thanksgiving sandwiched in the middle. Mom deserved at least that much. Lily would make a holiday dinner that none of them would forget. Hopefully, in a good way.

Even without C.J.'s help.

She frowned at one of the sliding doors that led to the traveler-pickup area. Had she expected him to rush to her aid after the way she'd ended things between them?

More bags entered the circuit, their owners popping out of line to nab them. If her luggage didn't show, she could just borrow something from—

She stopped herself, blinking hard. A knot swelled in her throat. How could she have forgotten, for even a moment? Mom was gone. Lily had always thought there would be more time to fix their broken relationship. More time to make things right.

She had been wrong.

No, she couldn't think about that now. Not if she hoped to make it to Brighton tonight. She glanced back to the carousel just as her bright-purple bag popped out. But as she clasped the satchel's handles and bent her knees to heft it off the belt, a black-leather-covered arm reached around her and yanked it from her hand.

"Hey, that's mine!"

Lily whipped around, prepared to battle with her bag thief, but she found herself looking into the open collar of a white dress shirt that peeked out from an unzipped leather jacket. She took a step back and tilted her head up to get a glimpse of the crook with good fashion sense.

C.J. Grayson looked down at her, the right side of his mouth lifting. "Hey, Lil."

She could only stare back at him as other travelers stepped past them to collect their bags. No matter what he'd said when she'd called and begged him before, he was here now. Even if he looked more like the guy from that Boston Back Bay restaurant website than the kid who used to wrestle her brothers on their parents' family-room rug. But he was thirty now, and a lot could change in six years.

His mop of dark-brown hair was trimmed so short that his curls had mellowed to waves. His baby face had harder lines than she remembered, too, and those were a perfect match for the close-trimmed mustache and beard he wore now. Only his deep-brown eyes looked the same. They were every bit as opaque and intense as they'd always been.

"You came," she somehow managed.

"I came." He plunked her bag on the floor close to her feet. "But only because I need something from you, too."

"What do you mean?"

C.J. reached for his own wheeled carry-on with a computer bag on top and settled it next her satchel. His suitcase was trim and tidy, and hers had more battle scars than a two-war vet. Kind of like the two of them, though she wasn't about to tell *him* that.

"You're getting free cooking assistance from a chef for Thanksgiving dinner. I think I should get something, too. Like some photos for my social-media platforms."

Photos of her family on the first holiday since her mother's death? She shook her head. "That doesn't seem like a good idea—"

"Want my help or not?"

"But why *my* family?"

C.J., who'd never been the argumentative type before, crossed his arms over his chest.

"That's my condition. You need to make a holiday dinner without giving your family food poisoning, and I need a family—I mean a *big* family—for some publicity shots."

"Okay, I guess. As long as the others agree."

"They'll agree."

"Will you be bringing in a photographer?"

He shook his head. "It's social media. Cell-phone photos will be fine."

She nodded, though his plan sounded different from her own experience in L.A., where even the dishwashers had professional headshots. Without asking for permission, C.J. lifted her bag again, grabbed the handle for his and headed for the exit. She was left with no choice but to skitter after him.

"How did you get my flight arrangements, anyway?"

"You told me when you begged me to come."

Right. She had. "I can carry my own luggage, you know."

"I know." But he kept walking.

Frowning, she followed with just her cross-shoulder purse at her side.

"Thanks for doing this."

He stopped but didn't look at her. "I didn't do it for you. I did it for Mama Monroe."

As if that settled the matter, C.J. started forward again. Good thing he didn't ask her a question because she couldn't speak over the emotion clogging her throat. He was the only one who'd used that nickname for her mother. The rest of her brothers' friends, and hers, had called Penny Monroe some derivative of "Lieutenant," since everyone had been impressed that she was a ranking officer with the Michigan State Police. Everyone, at least, except her daughter.

"Well, thanks, anyway. For *her*."

"Also, I've tasted your cooking."

She chuckled. "That's fair."

C.J. stopped again and looked at her this time. "I was sorry to hear about your mom. How long has it been?"

"Thanks. Eight weeks."

"Still pretty recent."

"It was fast, too. Less than a month from diagnosis."

She tried to push away the image of her formerly-vibrant mother in that hospital bed, with painkillers holding her in that merciful limbo between agony and death.

"Mamma Monroe was an amazing lady."

She nodded, her eyes burning. If she started crying now, she

4

might never stop.

"I wanted to come to the funeral, but you know how it is in the restaurant business. Hard to get away."

"I can imagine. The flowers you sent were lovely though."

And as much of a surprise as his words were. He'd wanted to attend the funeral? Even as uncomfortable as it might have been? Come to think of it, if he hadn't been able to schedule time off for that, then how had he managed it during a holiday week?

"What now?" she asked, then wished she hadn't. This was her gig. She should have been directing. But she'd never thought beyond that first crazy idea of asking C.J. for his culinary backup. Make that the *second* crazy idea. The first was volunteering to make the family Thanksgiving dinner when her cooking repertoire was limited to soup from a can and mac-and-cheese *a la box*.

"Do you have a rental car, or is one of your brothers picking you up?"

"I'd planned to order a RideNow."

"It's over forty miles to Brighton."

He clearly didn't believe her lie about the ride-sharing service. Had he also figured out that she was planning to wing this whole trip, just as she had her acting career? Look how well that had turned out.

"We'll take my rental." He pointed to the sign for short-term parking and held up a set of keys on a long plastic keychain. "I picked it up earlier."

As Lily followed him out the door and across the crosswalk to the parking garage, the frigid Michigan wind pushed open the sides of her canvas jacket and blew her hair across her face.

She was still shivering and finger-combing her tangles when they entered the elevator.

"I barely recognized you with that hair," he said as the

doors closed.

"What?" Self-conscious now, she shoved it out of her eyes once more and lowered her hand.

He frowned, as if he regretted mentioning it.

"Oh. You mean the color," she said. "Yeah, no more purple or orange or pink. Apparently, *edgy* doesn't get many roles, so, I'm back to ordinary blond now."

Twenty-eight was a little old for rainbow, protest hair as well, but she kept that to herself.

"It looks different."

Well, it wasn't a glowing review, but he hadn't been as unkind as he could have been. Meanness was as plentiful as out-of-work actors in L.A.

"Thanks for the ride," she said as she stared at the numbers above the elevator door. "You can drop me off on the way to your mom's."

"Didn't you know? Mom moved to Pasadena with her new husband almost three years ago."

"No, I didn't." In fact, she didn't know much about him that couldn't be found out from an Internet search and his restaurant's website. What she *could* tell, though, was that he hadn't spent much time alone.

"So you'll be staying…?" she asked as the doors opened.

"With you, I thought."

Lily swallowed as C.J. gestured for her to go ahead. Of course, he hadn't meant anything as graphic as the image that crept into her thoughts. They'd never even kissed in her childhood bedroom with its mint-green ruffles and lace. That truth didn't stop other moments, some steamy, some tender, from waltzing through her memory. She shouldn't think of those now. He was only in town as a favor. Nothing more. She couldn't afford to remember. Or wish.

"I mean, if there's room at your folks' place…"

He let his words trail away as if he didn't already know the answer. Even with the whole family in town, they could find space for one more. What the Georgian colonial lacked in amenities and updates of any kind, it made up for in its sprawling size.

"We can find a place for you."

"I can even sleep on the floor, if you can spare a few blankets. It will be easier if I'm staying there to do all the cooking, anyway."

Lily was the only one making a big deal about him being a guest in her parents' house.

"It will be a nice chance for you to get to see Phil and Peter, too. How long has it been?"

He clicked his key fob, and the taillights on a crossover SUV flicked on. "How long has it been since you dumped me? Oh. Right. Six years."

Lily's breath caught, and she coughed into her elbow to cover it.

C.J. raised the hatch and stowed their bags in the back before rounding the car to driver's side. "Coming?"

Lily climbed in the passenger side. She was grateful for the silence as he pulled out of the garage. She needed time to recover. She'd held the silly hope that for the whole week no one would mention the woolly mammoth in the room that was their past relationship. Instead, C.J. had lobbed it straight at her and let her in on some information at the same time.

Had the twins broken contact with C.J. out of loyalty to her? Especially when she'd broken up with *him*. Her heart ached that he might have lost his girlfriend and his two best friends the same day. Even if she'd left him for all the right reasons.

She peeked at his dark profile as he followed the signs for Interstate 275. Would he ever believe that she'd broken up with him for his own good? Maybe not, but C.J. hadn't watched her father give up his dreams to support her mother's state police career. Or been a spectator as her father lost himself in the process.

She'd been determined not to let that happen to C.J. Had refused to let him lose his culinary dreams to help her reach her acting ones. She'd worried he would have become a shadow to her spotlight. He would have, too. So she couldn't be sorry, no matter how things had turned out.

It was the most unselfish thing she'd ever done. For in addition to being the strong woman everyone loved and admired, her mother had also been overly ambitious and sometimes blind to anyone's needs but her own. How could she explain to a guy who'd always adored her mother that the woman also had faults? How could Lily tell him that she'd been afraid she would turn out just like her?

Chapter 2

T Minus 65 Hours

C.J. PARKED ALONG the side of the dimly lit gravel driveway and then gripped the steering wheel as tightly as he had for most of the trip back to Brighton. He tried to keep his focus on the dark line of cars parked near the barn and the darker backdrop of evergreens against an indigo sky beyond them, but it wasn't a fair fight. If he hadn't been able to keep from watching Lily when he should have been concentrating on the road to keep them alive, he didn't stand a chance now.

Who was he kidding? From the moment she'd spun around to face him in the airport, her pale blue eyes even prettier now without all that heavy black gunk she used to wear to outline them, he hadn't been able to see anything *except* her.

He'd already let slip that he'd noticed her hair, with its long silky strands that weren't close to "ordinary," but he hadn't missed anything else, either. The delicate line of her chin, that dainty upturned nose and those lips with their more dramatic peaks and valleys. The petite, perfect body that a man might want to spend the rest of his life holding in his arms each night.

He pitied any sucker who ever thought that about Lily. Or was foolish enough to propose to her.

Like C.J. once had.

"Well, we're here," she said but didn't open the door.

C.J. blinked several times, caught with his thoughts in forbidden territory.

"That was the plan, right?"

"Guess so." Still, she didn't move.

"Your family is probably anxious for us—I mean you—to go in, so…?" That there were enough lights on inside for the house to be visible from an altitude of two-thousand feet and no one had come out to greet them by now made him wonder about that.

He turned back to find her with her arm braced against the door handle, the same uncomfortable position she'd been in most of the drive from the airport. He had to squeeze the steering wheel even tighter to keep from reaching out to comfort her.

This had to stop. He was supposed to be immune to Lily now. Hadn't he inoculated himself while sharing revolving delights with some of the most beautiful women along the East Coast? Lily was supposed to be just a blip in his dating history. A beginner's mistake, even if that blunder lasted two years. But he'd been in the car with her less than an hour, the melding scents of jasmine and peach refusing to stay on her side, and his thoughts were traveling down a memory lane that should have been wiped off the map.

Returning to Michigan was a mistake. He refused to call it coming back to *her*. He should have kept at least a three-state buffer between them instead of canceling his smart refusal and then turning her family dinner into a publicity stunt for the restaurant. But he was here now, and he'd made a promise. Like any other crisis in the kitchen, he could handle it if he just stayed in control.

"Let's get inside. We need to start work tonight."

"Wait. What?" She turned to look at him. "But it's only Monday."

"Which means we have just over two days of prep until show time. We need menu cards. Place cards. Centerpieces." He tapped the steering wheel with each item he listed.

"Menu cards? Place cards? Whoa! Aren't we going a little overboard here? This isn't a dinner party. It's just family. We know everyone's names. Can't we make some turkey and stuffing and call it done?"

"You could have done that without my help."

"Are you sure about that?" She blew out a breath. "Fine. Maybe I could have, as long as the fire department was on call."

"I'll ask it again. Do you want my help or not?"

She shifted next to him as if he'd surprised her. No, he wasn't the easygoing guy she remembered. That guy didn't exist anymore. He'd grown up. He'd figured out that no one got everything he wanted in life, and he was trying to be content with his share.

"Yes...I need your help."

Now he was the one straightening in his seat. She needed him, and no matter what he'd said before, at least part of the reason he'd come was probably because she did. But there was no way he would admit that to her, at least not without advanced interrogation techniques.

"I'm glad that's settled," he said instead. "Now, if *Christopher's* name is going to be attached to this event, and there will be photos, we can't serve deli turkey breast and jellied cranberry sauce out of a can."

"Guess not."

She glanced back to the house, as if she, too, expected someone to finally notice that they'd arrived.

But then she turned back to him. "Hey, you're *Christopher*. Why do you talk about yourself in the third-person?"

"It's the restaurant's name. As for me, I'm still trying it on." He wasn't sure he would ever get used to seeing it on the restaurant sign.

"But haven't you been open for two years? And wasn't it named 'Best of Boston' for your clam chowder or something?"

He couldn't help smiling into the darkness this time. Even if she'd only looked up his contact information to sponge off his cooking skills, Lily had been stalking him on the Internet. All the details he knew about her, from commercials and bit parts to the long stretches between acting roles of any kind, would be harder for him to explain.

"Okay then, *Captain, my captain.*" She waved a hand toward him. "I'll do it your way. Just give me detailed instructions. I am your willing...*sous chef.*"

Since he'd already coughed before she'd spoken the last two words, he made a show of looking out the window toward the house again. He had no business imagining that she might be his willing *anything else.*

"You'll have to earn that title," he managed. "You haven't even made it to prep cook yet."

"It's a wonder you keep any employees when you talk to people like that." She sighed. "Fine. Just give me my list of assignments, and I'll do them."

"*Any* assignments?"

The words came out before he could stop himself. He hoped she would miss his innuendo, or at least pretend to.

After a long pause, she said, "Within reason."

"Good. Because pulling that bag with the neck, heart and gizzards from inside the turkey carcass can get pretty gross."

"You're not going to make me do all the nastiest parts, are you?"

"No, I wouldn't do that." He opened the car door because it was becoming clear that she would stall all night if he let her. "But do you remember how many times Mama Monroe tried to get you into the kitchen so she could pass down family recipes?"

Though she opened her door, she still didn't climb out. "Too many to count, I guess."

"Well, her method might be unconventional, but I think your mom finally has you right where she wants you."

"You think so?"

She met his gaze now, hers pleading for forgiveness that wasn't his to give. It was a reminder that he wasn't the only one Lily might have hurt.

"I do," he said anyway. "And in her honor, I'm going to make sure you finally learn how to cook."

Chapter 3

T Minus 64 Hours and 30 Minutes

LILY REACHED FOR the front door handle and then pulled back her hand as if reconsidering. A knot formed in C.J.'s throat as Lily rang the bell instead. Unlike his old house that was probably on its second owner since his mom had unloaded it, Lily's childhood home was still here, filled with people she loved. Only it wasn't *her* home anymore.

Her brother pulled open the door and stepped aside to let her enter. "Sis, I keep telling you not to ring—"

"How's it going, Phil?" C.J. said as he followed her inside. Though the twins were identical, sandy-haired linebackers, he'd always been able to tell them apart. At least one thing hadn't changed.

"Grayson? What the hell are *you* doing here?"

C.J. managed to set his bag and the one he'd wrenched from Lily's hand on the worn parquet flooring before Phil grabbed him in a bear hug.

"Did I hear you say Grayson?" Peter called out just as his brother released C.J. He barreled into the front hall, grabbed C.J. around the waist and lifted him right off the floor.

He was grinning when his shoes touched down again. Man, he'd missed this. Missed this family, this place and his twin best friends who'd dwarfed him with their massive size. Whose little sister he'd once loved so much he couldn't breathe.

"I know where I rank."

Almost as one, Phil and Peter whirled to find their sister standing next to the closet.

"Hey, Daffodil!" Peter called out as he crossed to her.

Lily frowned over his use of one of the many nicknames the twins had found for a younger sister named after a flower, but she let him hug her anyway.

Phil stepped closer for his turn to give her a squeeze. "Well, Daisy, we weren't ever going to say anything about liking this guy better, but now that you've figured it out…"

"Hold up," Peter interrupted his twin the way he'd done since they were kids before turning to their sister. "You brought C.J. home for Thanksgiving? You're not back…?"

At least he hadn't said the word *together*. Lily probably would have passed out on the floor if he had. She was already staring at her shoes and looking so guilty that if their mom had still been alive, she would have slapped handcuffs on her for suspicious behavior. Lily deserved every second of this awkwardness if she hadn't planned out what she would tell her family when she showed up with him, and yet he couldn't help trying to rescue her. Again.

"Didn't she tell you?"

The twins' curious expressions were nothing compared to the wide-eyed look Lily tossed his way. Did she expect him to humiliate her?

"You see, I needed to do some publicity for the restaurant, so I begged her to let me come to Thanksgiving dinner." He needed to slow down, or everyone would know that he was making up his story as he went along. "I thought your family would be perfect for the project."

Peter burst out laughing. "Perfect? Have you met *us*?"

"Well, it's a big family, anyway," C.J. said.

Peter's face sobered. "I guess it still is."

"Yeah, I'm sorry about your mom."

The brothers thanked him in that stilted way men have of acknowledging a comment and announcing that they don't want to talk about it.

"So...," Phil said, "when you say 'come to Thanksgiving dinner,' is that code for *cook*?"

"You'll be making dinner instead of Tulip here?" Peter brushed the backside of his hand over his forehead. "Whew! We were terrified when she announced that she would be cooking."

"I *will* be cooking," Lily said, crossing her arms. "He's just...helping out."

Her brothers nodded and winked as if they'd choreographed the move.

"I can't remember last time you even showed up for one of our family holiday dinners," Phil noted.

Lily opened her mouth to answer and then closed it again.

"It's been a while for me, too," C.J. piped in, and they all nodded. No one needed to mention that their mom had included him in some of their dinners when his own mother had found nothing to celebrate in the years following his dad's death.

"Well, are you guys okay with being a part of my publicity stunt?" he asked after a long pause.

"Do we get to be on TV?" Peter patted the twin peaks of his receding hairline.

C.J. shook his head. "Nothing that dramatic. Just some shots for my blog and website."

Phil's gaze narrowed. "Are we going to have to get dressed up? Because I need to wear my lucky Detroit Lions jersey for the game."

"You can't throw on a sweater for one hour?"

Peter socked his brother's shoulder. "Sure, he can."

C.J. turned back to Peter. "You're on board, but shouldn't I ask the others?"

Lily looked down the hall and then toward the stairs. "Where is everyone, anyway? Is Dad spending all his time in his bedroom? And where's Roy?" She glanced around for the aging Border collie mix. "He didn't even bark."

"Roy's in Dad's room, sleeping off too much playing with the kids. Poor old boy," Peter told them. "And Dad's out. At painting class, I think."

Phil squinted and tapped his lips with his index finger. "No. It's Monday, so it's Photography Club."

Lily nodded. "That's right. He told me he's been trying to get out more. What about Debbie and Tina?"

"Putting the kids to bed." Peter slid a look toward the stairs and then spoke in a conspiratorial voice. "The ladies have their panties in a bunch about the dinner. You might want to tread lightly."

"You mean because I'm cooking?" Lily asked. "Why would that upset them?"

"Who do you think helped Mom put all the holiday dinners together when you *weren't* here?"

"You guys maybe?"

"Hardly." Phil chuckled. "We were banned from the kitchen after the grease-fire incident. Don't ask."

Lily rolled her eyes. "I won't. But I didn't mean to put anyone out. I just wanted to do something...for Mom."

This time Peter stepped close and wrapped an arm around his sister's shoulders. "Don't worry about the ladies. They'll get over it. But I wouldn't be too shocked if they short-sheeted the bed in your room."

"Speaking of rooms, which one can C.J. have?" she asked. "He needs to stay here since his mom moved to California."

Phil shook his head. "We'd love to help, but there's no room in the inn."

Lily held her hands wide. "This house has *five* bedrooms."

Phil counted on his fingers. "One for dad. One for Tina, the baby and me. Another for Debbie and Peter. Another with three kids stacked in it. You're lucky we saved one for *you*."

C.J. waved a hand to dismiss the problem. "No worries. I told you I could sleep on the floor."

"Why would you do that?" Phil said mildly. "When you can bunk with Petunia here."

"No," C.J. said.

But Lily's "absolutely not" was so loud and so sharp that it drowned him out. Her gaze connected with his for a few heartbeats, but she looked away. That her reaction annoyed him was just another reminder that he should never have left Boston. How many bad decisions could he make when it came to Lily Monroe? This was like a layover in Purgatory.

Phil was grinning when C.J. looked back to him.

"What's the big deal? It wouldn't be the first time." He waggled his eyebrows.

"Knock it off," Lily grumbled. Then she pointed down the hall. "There's a couch in the family room."

"Evan's already called it," Peter said, speaking of the son from his quick and brief first marriage. "He usually sleeps in Lily's room. Do you want to deal all week with the twelve-year-old whose *second* bed you've taken?"

"Not me." C.J. didn't have kids, but that still sounded like a bad idea.

"And don't suggest the living room couch," Phil added. "I can't even sit on that thing more than five minutes without getting a butt ache."

"Lily, do you really think that Mom would have been okay with a guest sleeping on the floor?"

Peter asked the question, but both brothers stared her down with their disappointed expressions.

C.J. held his hands wide. "Hey, guys. I'll just get a hotel. We passed at least three near the Grand River exit."

"Or making a guest get a hotel?" Phil continued his brother's question.

"Fine," Lily spat with an exasperated sigh. "He can stay in my room."

C.J. swallowed. How was he supposed to sleep with her in the same room, breathing the same air, let alone in the same *bed* with her? Even if he'd sworn off ever touching her again, nothing less than a lobotomy would have let him forget how soft her skin was. How perfectly they'd fit. His skin tingled with taboo memories.

Forget Purgatory, this was a vacation in Hell.

Without looking at him or at her sniggering brothers, Lily marched to their suitcases by the door, lifted her own and headed to the stairs.

C.J. lumbered after her, a frustrating throwback to the time when he'd chased after her with a same futility as a child losing hold on a helium balloon. Now he was tempted to turn and stomp to the door, not stopping until he could smell sautéing vegetables and wine reductions in his restaurant kitchen. But he followed her, anyway.

Lily was halfway up the stairs and he'd just reached the bottom when she looked back at him over her shoulder.

"You get the trundle bed," she said. "And if I hear one snore, you're out in the hall."

Chapter 4

"SHE'S HERE! SHE'S here!"

At the mix of shrill voices and the crack of the door against something solid, Lily's eyes popped open. Where was she? Why was she still so tired? She rubbed her gritty eyes. But before she could make sense of her surroundings with only the light streaming in through the open door, something pounded across the room and landed in a lump on top of her feet.

Make that two lumps.

"Aunt Lily, it's morning," reported her five-year-old niece, Avery.

"Did we wake you up?" four-year-old Sidney asked.

"I think you did." She chuckled as the pieces fell into place.

The first Thanksgiving without Mom. Only two-and-a-half days to make a dinner that would rock her family's holiday table. Her tiny twin bed…with the trundle for friends.

Her throat tightened as she peeked in the direction she'd pushed that second bed last night, as far as humanly possible from hers in that too-narrow room. But the bed was empty now, the sheets straightened, blankets folded at the bottom. Where had C.J. gone? And a more important question than that, how had she slept, even a few minutes, with him lying there, not six feet away from her?

Something clicked near the door then, and the whole room was filled with light. Already dressed in jeans and an open flannel shirt over a navy T-shirt, C.J. sat at her desk, a pen and notepad in his hands. Purple shadows beneath his eyes suggested he hadn't slept much last night, either.

"Girls, I think you interrupted Aunt Lily's beauty sleep."

He grinned, his look so warm and steady that heat spread from her chest to her face. She lowered her gaze and got a close-up look at the flimsy camisole she'd paired with her pajama pants. One that practically outlined her curves with a black marker.

As she tucked the comforter under her armpits, she couldn't help but noticing the fuzzy tan blanket spread on top of the others. He'd clearly taken the time to cover her in the night. She didn't know what to make of that. She expected him to be waiting for her reaction, but her nieces had his full attention as they scooted off her bed and padded toward him.

"Who are you?" Avery wanted to know.

"I'm your aunt's friend, C.J. Who are you?"

At his words, Lily's chest felt tight. *Friends.* If only that were true. At least that.

"I'm Avery."

"I'm Sidney."

"Why are you here?" Avery asked.

C.J. did look at Lily this time. He must have wondered the same thing the child had asked.

Her nieces would have kept right on peppering the stranger in her bedroom with questions, but someone marched up the steps.

"Girls, if you're in Aunt Lily's room, you're going to be in big trouble."

The voice belonged to one of her sisters-in-law, though Lily wasn't sure which. Giggling, her nieces scampered out before they could be caught. They left the door open, but that didn't stop the air in that small space from feeling as thin as it had the night before.

"Are they twins?" C.J. asked as he watched them go.

"Cousins."

"Even better." He paused for a few seconds and then added, "The more family the better for my blog photos."

Lily suspected there might be more to what he'd said, but she played along anyway.

"Then you should thank my brothers and sisters-in-law for their fertility. Peter and Debbie have four kids, three boys and a girl. Phil and Tina are trailing behind with just two girls."

"They've got some catching up to do."

Though C.J.'s laptop was still on the corner of the desk, where he'd plugged it in the night before, he started writing again in the pad of paper he'd taken from her desk drawer.

"What are you doing over there?"

He showed her a grocery list that would empty the shelves of the local supermarket. "We didn't get to this last night, so we're already behind."

"We needed to get some sleep." Or at least she needed to *pretend* she was sleeping, so she could avoid having to face questions she couldn't answer. Those were the same things, weren't they? "Were you working in the dark?"

He flipped the flashlight on his cell phone on and off and then set it aside.

"I didn't want the laptop to wake you. Anyway, I figured you could use some extra sleep since I'm about to wear you out today." He shifted. "In the kitchen."

This time he sat stock-still. "You know what I mean."

"Yeah. I know."

But she couldn't stop her hands from becoming damp or the nervous giggle that chased after her words. The problem was that she knew too many things about him. Like how his head tilted to the right when he told anything less than the absolute truth. Like how his heart seemed to beat beneath *her* skin when he held her close.

C.J. ripped off his list with an almost angry tear.

"Hurry up and get dressed, so we can go to the store. We're wasting valuable daylight hours."

She drew her brows together. "Um…okay."

Discreetly, she wiped her hands on the blanket he'd stretched over her earlier. But he didn't even look back as he stuffed the paper into his jeans pocket and stepped out of the room. The door closed with a final-sounding *click*. A few seconds later, she could hear his footsteps on the stairs.

Lily stared at the closed door for a few seconds and then climbed out of bed and smoothed the blankets. She dressed and tied her hair back in a low ponytail. Then she headed down the hall to brush her teeth and wash her face.

If only it were as easy for her to wipe thoughts of C.J. from her mind. Sure, she'd asked him to help her make the dinner for her family, but had she also secretly wished for a chance to be with him, even if just for a short while?

Yes, she'd pushed him away. For his own good. But he was the only man who'd ever given her sweaty palms. The only one she'd ever loved. Though she'd carried him in her heart all this time, it was clear now that he wasn't pining for her.

For him at least, they were truly over. She would just have to learn to live with that.

Chapter 5

"LOOK WHO'S AWAKE and already cooking up a storm this morning."

Lily glanced over from the ironing board where she was *not* cooking, storm or otherwise. Her father, Garrett Monroe, stood in the wide kitchen doorway, dressed in a faded Detroit Pistons zipper sweatshirt and sweatpants.

"Hi, Dad. Morning's almost over. We've been working on the dinner for hours."

If shopping for groceries, dinnerware and table linens, ironing napkins that would later be folded into turkey shapes and ordering centerpieces with the biggest curmudgeon of an instructor she'd even met counted as *working on the dinner*, anyway. C.J. had barked orders all morning and snapped at her every time she asked a question. Okay, she'd made a few comments of her own, but didn't a gal have the right to defend herself?

"I don't see any pumpkin pies yet," Garrett noted.

"Give us time," she said.

If she had to spend *more time* working with C.J., one of them might be as dead as the free-range turkey they'd scheduled for delivery tomorrow. Probably C.J. But she didn't tell her father that. Instead, she set the iron aside and crossed the room to kiss his cheek.

Had his face looked that ruddy the last time she'd seen him? Since they'd last been together for the funeral, she shouldn't make any comparisons, but he looked thinner, too. Had he kept something about his own health from her while he'd been caring for her mother? She took another look at his slovenly clothes. Was he still wearing his pajamas?

"You didn't just get up, did you?" she asked. "It's nearly noon."

Her father glanced down at his sweatshirt and laughed. "It wouldn't be a big deal if I'd just rolled out of bed. I'm a grown-up, after all. But I was at the gym. Marcie's ten-o'clock spin class is a killer. I was helping set up a show at the gallery before that."

He unzipped his sweatshirt to reveal a sweat-soaked T-shirt and then shoved his hand back through his damp salt-and-pepper hair.

"Spin class? Gallery?" Her mouth must have been hanging open because C.J. stepped forward and eased her out of the way.

"Hello, Mr. Monroe." He extended his hand, and Garrett gripped it. "It's great that you're staying busy."

She would have said something like that herself if she'd been on her toes that morning. Still, her father frowned at C.J.

"We've known each other, son, for…what? Twenty years? Don't you think it's time you called me Garrett?"

"Uh…sure," C.J. said. "I was sorry to hear about Mrs. Monroe."

"I appreciate that." Garrett lowered his gaze to the floor, but when he looked up again, he was smiling. "My wife always had nice things to say about you."

Now C.J. was the one staring at the kitchen tile. "Thanks, Mr. Monroe." He cleared his throat. "I mean…Garrett."

Her father took in the stacked boxes, bottles and cans they'd purchased that morning. Things that didn't come close to fitting in the pantry. Lily squirmed just as she had while watching the cashier scan the items and praying her credit limit could take the hit. She'd refused to let C.J. pay for the groceries. Especially after he'd already insisted on buying the new white dishes and the fancy linens he needed for his photos.

"You two cooking for the whole neighborhood?" He looked at C.J. instead of his daughter.

"Lily just wants to make it special for all of you."

"It's good that she has you to help her." Garrett wrapped his hands around a ten-pound bag of flour.

"No one else seems to be stepping up to help her."

C.J. pointed to the kitchen doorway that no one had passed through since they'd returned with the groceries and dishes two hours before. They wouldn't have seen her brothers, sisters-in-law and nieces and nephews at all if the others hadn't stuck their heads in to say hello that morning on the way out the door.

"Can't say as I blame 'em."

Lily had just sneaked a peek at C.J., surprised that he'd defended her after the tense morning they'd just spent, but her father's words shocked her even more.

"What's that supposed to mean?"

Garrett chuckled. "From what I hear, there's been nothing but bickering going on in here."

Lily and C.J. traded glances and looked away. The rumor mill had called that one right.

"The guys are probably laying low so they won't be drafted into a war zone, and the gals are hanging back because of their wounded pride." Garrett grinned again. "You did all but throw them out of the kitchen."

"It wasn't like that," Lily said.

26

"For you, maybe."

Finally, she nodded.

"And the fact that they're keeping all the kids and one hungry dog from under your feet while you work, well, consider that a gift."

"But I love the kids. And Roy."

"Don't worry. You'll get your fill of them later." He patted her shoulder. "I wouldn't worry about the grown-ups, either. They'll come around."

"I'm sure they will." Lily wasn't as confident as he appeared to be. She'd thought her broken relationship had been with her mother alone, but maybe she'd written herself out of the whole family album without realizing it.

She glanced back at her father and found him watching her. "You're so much like her."

A knot forming in her throat, Lily shook her head. He probably thought he was complimenting her.

"Sure, you two knocked heads, but you had a lot in common. I just wish—" Garrett stopped himself and closed his eyes for a few seconds.

C.J. cleared his throat. "Well, unless you're okay with peanut butter sandwiches for Thanksgiving dinner, we'd better get back to work."

"You're right." Garrett started toward the door, but as he passed C.J., he paused. "I wish she'd had the chance to see this."

Lily was curious what her father meant by *this*, but she didn't dare ask. C.J. didn't take the same precaution.

"Yeah, Mama Monroe would have loved to finally see Lily in the kitchen," he said.

"It's more than that." Garrett indicated them both with a sweep of his hand. "She was right when she said that our girl made a big mistake when she let you get away."

Chapter 6

C.J. STOOD FROZEN with his hands braced on the counter as he watched Garrett's retreating form. Realizing his mouth was hanging open, he clamped it shut. There was nothing he could do about his racing heart. He was dying to see Lily's face, but he couldn't look because it would give her the chance to see his.

Talk about tossing a grenade and then sprinting for safer ground. Lily's dad couldn't have made a hastier retreat after lobbing that one. *Let you get away.* The words kept replaying in his thoughts like one of his mom's old forty-five records as it skipped on a scratch.

Had Lily's mom really said that about him? It was both sweet and naive, but he hadn't expected Lily to tell her mother the truth. Her daughter hadn't *let* him get away. She'd shoved him and the engagement ring he'd bought away with one hand while applying lipstick with the other for a date with some dude.

Maybe it was better that Penny Monroe would never know how her daughter had broken off their relationship.

"Sorry," Lily said from behind him.

C.J. straightened. It was as if she'd slipped inside his thoughts and was responding to his complaint. Her apology shouldn't matter now. Too much time had passed. Still, he heard himself asking, "For what?"

"For that."

She pointed at the doorway through which her father had disappeared. Then she tucked her hands behind her and leaned against the counter.

"Talking about your dad? He means well."

"No, it's more than that," she said. "I'm sorry for bringing you here. To them. When none of them know the whole story."

"You mean that you were the dumper and not the *dumpee*? Or that you had another guy for a nice parachute landing?"

She stared down at her tennis shoe and skimmed her foot back and forth on the floor. "I told them it was mutual."

"Was it?"

For several seconds, she said nothing. They both knew it was anything *but* mutual. One of them had seen something between them that hadn't actually been there.

"I'm sorry about how things went down."

It was a sanitized way of describing the thing she'd done, but he nodded anyway.

"It's the past. Water under the bridge." That didn't mean the bridge hadn't been shaken all the way through its pilings, but he wasn't about to tell her that. "We've both moved on. I know I have."

"Right." Lily stepped back to the ironing board, the light on the iron blinking to show its heat had shut off. She flipped it back on before adding, "I saw the photos."

"You've been following my love life online?"

"No." She stretched one of the last few cloth napkins across the board and started smoothing its wrinkles. "I just saw a few things when I was trying to track you down. You know, for this." She indicated the mess in the kitchen. "But you're something of a celebrity Casanova now."

He waited for her to deliver a punch line, but she kept her back to him as she continued to work. Had it bothered her to see him with other women? Should he give a damn if it did?

"It's not as exciting as all that," he said anyway. "They're pretty starved for celebrities in the Back Bay area, so my social life gets some unwanted attention."

He grabbed the bag of fresh cranberries that he'd left out when they'd stuffed most of the produce into her family's side-by-side refrigerator. "Do you think your dad's right? Has it really sounded like a war zone in here?"

"Maybe. Is your kitchen at *Christopher's* loud like that, too?"

"Sometimes." Mostly when the sous chef, the pantry cook and the wine steward got into it, but that wouldn't support his point about the noise in Lily's house, so he didn't say more.

"Are you as tough on your employees as you've been on me?"

"Sometimes," he answered again. "But only when they're messing up."

"Am I messing up?"

"No." Other than to ask him to come here and pop open this can of old wounds that should have remained vacuum-sealed for eternity, she hadn't done anything wrong.

"Then why—"

"Look," he interrupted her before she could ask a question he couldn't answer. "Why don't we start over? I told you I would help you for your mom's sake. And for my blog. I can also be a little nicer while we're working together."

"Me, too," she said, though technically her behavior had been better than his. She indicated the pile of ironed table linens. "Want to show me how to make turkey shapes with the napkins now?"

"How about we take a break from the prep stuff and do

some actual cooking?"

"You said most of the stuff would have to be made tomorrow and Thursday."

"That's right. But there are a few things we can make today before we go to the printer to pick out the stationery." He pointed to the bag of cranberries in his hand. "Like cranberry sauce."

She dug through several cabinets, as much a stranger in this kitchen as he was, until she located the thick-bottomed saucepan he'd requested.

"Are you sure we can't just go back to the store for the stuff in the can? The jelly slices up real nice."

She was grinning, and he couldn't help smiling back at her. So easily she drew him in. Like always. It would have been safer to give orders like he had earlier, but he'd said he would be nicer, and at least one of them kept his promises.

"Once you taste this stuff, you'll never mention the can again."

When Lily stood, holding the saucepan by the handle, C.J. pressed the bag of berries into her other hand.

He made an open workspace on the counter and arranged in a line the cutting board, food chopper, bag of sugar, fresh mint leaves, an orange and containers of cinnamon sticks and nutmeg pods. After collecting measuring cups and spoons, he dug through one of the remaining grocery bags and retrieved the zester kitchen tool he'd insisted on buying earlier. He'd been right to guess that there wouldn't be one, even in Penny Monroe's well-appointed kitchen.

"All of that stuff goes into cranberry sauce?"

At his direction, she set the pan on the stove, ripped open the bag and dumped the cranberries in it.

"It does in mine. And now yours."

"Mine?"

"Did you think I would do all the cooking while you served as my helpful assistant, finding pans and bringing over measuring spoons?"

"No, I thought I would spend the next two days folding napkins."

"I can see that. But in cooking, you learn by doing, so you're going to be doing a lot of it." When she grimaced, he assured her, "I'll guide you each step of the way. Then when you serve up this meal, you can truly say *you* made it."

Without using a recipe, C.J. directed Lily as she measured ingredients and combined them in the pan. He demonstrated how to use the zester on the side of the orange and then moved out of her way so she could try it.

"Remember, you only want the outer, orange skin, not the white pith beneath it, or the food will taste bitter."

"No pressure there."

He had to smile as he watched her concentrating on the task. She looked more like a surgeon slicing into a frontal lobe than a cook scraping a fruit for its zest. When he grabbed his phone, she glanced over at him.

"What are you doing?"

C.J. shrugged as if he hadn't just been caught taking a cute photo of his old girlfriend. "Remember the promotion for my blog?"

"I thought it was supposed to be about you making Thanksgiving dinner for a big family."

"I never said that." Good thing he hadn't because it would have made it harder for him to tailor the story. "My blog will show that even a novice cook can make an amazing Thanksgiving dinner with a chef's flare."

"You mean a cook with a chef standing over her shoulder to offer step-by-step instructions."

"That wouldn't make for a great headline, would it?"

She shook her head. "Probably not."

"But the people reading the blog will have the recipes right there in front of them."

"I don't know." She added the zest to the other ingredients and then turned on the stove to bring the mixture to a boil. "You didn't say that your publicity stunt was going to be about *me.*"

"Does that change anything? You already agreed to let me photograph your whole family."

"But that was different," she said as she chopped the mint leaves. "That wasn't making fun of my incompetence in the kitchen."

"My post won't poke fun of your cooking. It will show the new things you've learned."

"You still should have told me."

"You're right. I should have. I'm sorry." He waited a few seconds before asking, "Are you still game?"

She shrugged and then nodded.

C.J. hated that he felt relieved. He couldn't have told her his plan for the blog, anyway, when he hadn't *planned* anything since she'd begged him to come to Michigan. But even he wasn't buying his story anymore that he'd come here for publicity...or even to honor Lily's mom. Those were justifications.

The real reason stood right before him, stirring a pan of cranberries and spices. She'd needed him to come, and he'd called in every favor he could to miss time at work and be there for her.

He was a glutton for punishment. He'd sworn he would never let any woman get close enough to burn him again, and here he was literally standing next to one by a hot stove.

And he wanted to step closer.

"I'm going to burn it. I burn everything."

C.J. leaned over and peered into the saucepan. "Not if you stir it occasionally, making sure you scrape the bottom of the pan, and you reduce the heat once it boils."

Lily's brows furrowed in concentration as she stirred more often than was necessary. He tried to stay focused on the food as well, on the safe place where the success or failure of a dish was usually within his control. But how was he supposed to keep his attention on the sauce when the hand that stirred it led to a shapely arm that curved over a rounded shoulder. And those were just a few of the places he longed to touch.

"Is it done yet?"

He blinked, interrupted from his long, slow simmer that had nothing to do with food. "It's up to you. Do *you* think it has thickened enough?"

She lifted the wooden spoon and let the sauce drip back into the pan.

"I think so."

"You're right." He directed her to move the sauce from the heating element and remove the nutmeg pod and cinnamon stick.

"You mean I did it?"

From her excitement he would have sworn she'd just made her first soufflé that didn't fall, but he couldn't help smiling anyway.

"Just put it in that nice glass bowl and let it cool before sprinkling on the mint."

She tipped the pan to pour it.

"Aren't you going to taste it first? Chefs always sample their dishes." He pulled a spoon from the silverware drawer and handed it to her.

She dipped the end of the spoon into the sauce and took a sip. Then she gestured toward her dish the way an auto show model might a brand-new Corvette.

"That stuff is amazing, and I made it."

"Yes, you did."

She poured the warm mixture into the bowl. "Okay, you helped, but I still cooked something that didn't come out of a box."

With each word, her voice grew louder until she sounded like one of her nieces as they'd slammed into her room that morning. Before C.J. realized what was happening, Lily had launched herself at him for a hug. He couldn't have stopped his arms from closing around her without the use of restraints. Muscle memory, senses and emotions long-buried conspired against him, their intent overwhelming his better judgment.

Like always, he was lost. In the sweet feel of her body pressed to his. In her scent. In everything about her.

C.J. could tell the moment Lily realized what she'd done because she froze. He lowered his hands to his sides.

"Sorry." She turned back to the dish. "I got a little excited."

He wouldn't touch that comment with a ten-foot wooden spoon. And if he had any sense at all, he would keep at least that much distance between them for the rest of his visit.

"You know what I mean."

He did, and yet he couldn't resist imagining things he had no business thinking about. If he wanted that to stop, he needed to concentrate on the job they had to do.

"If you're getting this carried away over making one dish, you're going to be worn out when you're on the twentieth one."

"Twenty different dishes?"

"Forget making Thanksgiving dinner, have you ever even *eaten* one?"

"Of course, I have."

"Then you know it's the national holiday of gluttony," he said. "Get ready. You have a lot of cooking to do."

Chapter 7

AS SHE PLODDED down the hall toward the stairs and, hopefully, sleep, exhaustion dragged on Lily's limbs like a sweatshirt worn in a swimming pool. She wasn't sure why she kept sipping coffee from the travel mug she carried. Caffeine had abandoned her brain hours before other than to leave her with trembling hands and an upset stomach.

Or maybe C.J. was to blame for both things.

Why had she done something stupid like hug him earlier? She wanted to call it an impulse, but she couldn't help wondering if she'd been craving this from the moment he'd shown up in the airport and had crash-landed back in her life.

"There are still a few pieces of pizza in those boxes in the family room. Want some more?"

C.J. spoke from a careful distance behind her, just as he'd kept a space barrier between them for the past several hours. So he wouldn't be forced to touch her again. As if the thought of it made his skin crawl or something.

She shook her head but kept walking. "The pepperoni already upset my stomach."

"Probably the coffee, too."

"You can eat some if you like."

"Nah, I'm not hungry."

36

Neither of them had eaten much all day, despite the tempting pizza her brothers had brought home earlier. Good thing Evan was a growing boy who could pick up the slack.

She'd just reached the bottom of the stairs when she glanced back and found him standing in the open doorway to her mother's home office. That room had been closed off the night before and earlier today, which had made it easier for her to pretend it didn't exist. Now its contents and the memories entwined with them seemed to burst into the hall.

"Hey, I remember this place." C.J. stepped inside and then glanced back at her. "Your mom's Michigan State Police room."

Her throat felt thick, and her stomach was even more unsettled than it had been before, but she found herself following him into the office, anyway. The plaques, the framed letters of commendation and recruit-class photographs looked the same as she remembered, but the glass case containing her mother's dress uniform hat and badge was new.

The memorabilia all but swirled around her, and the room's walls inched in, squeezing with a pressure that didn't make sense. She'd always hated everything the room represented— paramilitary structure and rules of the State Police and that it felt like her whole family had worked for the agency instead of only her mother. So why did every piece jab her heart now, producing a fresh ache?

C.J. approached the huge framed recruit photo and easily pointed out her mother in the group, though it had been taken years before he'd known her.

"She was proud of this place," he said. "I don't know how many times she walked me through it, pointing out all of her prized pieces."

Despite her discomfort, Lily smiled at the memory of it. "And you let her every time, even asking questions you already knew the answers to."

"She loved it." He moved on to the next photo.

"She loved *you*. Probably more than she did me." She'd meant it as a joke, but she couldn't hide the strain in her voice.

He looked back at her. "You don't believe that, do you? It isn't true."

"Maybe not, but I couldn't blame her if it were. I wasn't the easiest kid to raise." She cleared her throat. Why were they in this room, and why was she talking about memories that ripped open old wounds?

She waited for him to take her side the way he'd always done when they were together. This time he chuckled.

"You definitely put her through the paces. But then no one gets a guarantee of an easy job when becoming a parent."

She frowned. What had she expected him to do? Lie?

He crossed to her mother's desk and sat in the black-leather executive chair. Because it was easier than just standing there, Lily dropped onto the guest chair opposite the desk. It was the exact place she'd sat while her mother had given that speech about why she needed to choose a sensible major instead of something frivolous like theater. The words Lily had disregarded but had never forgotten.

C.J. leaned forward on the desk pad and reached for a gold frame positioned at the corner of the desk.

"She always loved you. Hard. You were lucky."

Even before he turned the frame toward her, Lily knew what she would see in that trio of small portraits. Her brothers stared back at her with bland picture-day smiles, and her twelve-year-old self looked out in adolescent misery. Though the photos on the staircase had always shown an age progression for all three of Penny Monroe's children, here in her office, the pictures remained the same, an awkward childhood phase frozen in time.

Lily had always wondered why her mother had never changed those photos, but now she couldn't help wondering if that period had been significant. Had the pictures shown a time when Penny still believed she could reach Lily?

"I just wasn't what she expected."

"Do you think she wanted you or one of your brothers to follow in her footsteps and go into law enforcement?"

"Not me." She shook her head. "Can you even imagine it?"

"No way."

"Anyway, Phil did sort of follow her path. He's an assistant prosecutor now."

"Right. He said that."

For a few seconds, C.J. didn't speak as he scanned the walls, his gaze pausing occasionally on a photo or plaque. But then he turned back to her.

"My mom didn't get what she expected, either."

He hadn't spoken of parenting when he'd mentioned his own mother, but there was no reason he should have. C.J. had been the kind of child any parent would have picked out from a catalog. If only his mother hadn't been so caught up in her grief over his father's sudden death that she couldn't recognize the gift she'd been given.

"How is your mom, anyway?"

"Good." He cleared his throat. "Happy."

He didn't say *finally*, but he might as well have. C.J. had been such a fixture in their house that Lily had never thought about how lonely it must have been for him in his own home, with a mother who was always around but never really there. Lily was ashamed now that she'd been too caught up in her own teenage drama to notice his pain.

"Your family had to be proud of all of this," C.J. said, returning to the earlier subject. He indicated the items on the room's four walls.

"I know I should have been. Many state police officers have a room like this in their houses. But I always hated it."

"Why is that?"

"Did you ever notice that Dad didn't have an office or a painting studio while Mom had all of this, and she wasn't even around half the time?"

"She was at work, supporting your family."

"I know that, but it always seemed like everything about our family revolved around her. *Her* career. *Her* promotions."

C.J. raised an eyebrow. "I never thought of you as anti-feminist."

"What do you mean by that?" She crossed her arms.

"How many families can you name where their whole dynamic and identity involves an orbit around the dad's career? Would it have bothered you as much if this had been your *father's* office? Your father's career?"

She shook her head. "It's not like that. It's just that…I don't know." Maybe he was right. Maybe she wouldn't have minded it if her family had followed the '60s TV-show, mom-in-an-apron-and-heels model, but that wasn't the point.

"My dad just got lost in the shuffle," she said. "He gave up everything for her. His art. Did you know he was supposed to take part in this traveling exhibition of Midwestern artists when I was about nine?"

"I don't remember that."

"That's because he turned it down. He told them they were welcome to include some of his acrylics in the exhibition, but he couldn't go. He said *someone* needed to be home in the evenings with us kids, and Mom was on afternoons, so…"

"He decided not to go," C.J. finished for her.

"But he didn't have a choice. Don't you see that?"

"No, but that's how you saw it."

She frowned at him. He was as difficult to get through to as her mother had been. "Just forget it."

"I will. There are a few things I'd like you to consider before I do though."

"Like what?"

"That your dad could have made a choice that he thought was best for your family. And possibly that he didn't regret his decision. He always seemed content with his life. Happy even."

"You don't know anything about it." The worst part was that he did seem to know. As if her mom was speaking to him through some otherworldly relay system. Or maybe he'd just had a good long talk with her dad. Either way, it was irritating her.

"You'll have to forgive me for being forward. I know I'm just the outsider that your family took pity on. But I still think you might not know the whole story."

"You don't know it either. And forward is right."

He shrugged. "But no one knows what goes on inside a marriage except the two people involved."

"And you've become this expert on marriage while dating every unattached woman in Massachusetts?" She pushed back the chair, stood and then stopped herself. "Look, I'm tired and annoyed and...I don't know what. We've got a ton of work left to do tomorrow. I'm going to bed."

She marched out of the room and then up the stairs. C.J. didn't follow, and she was glad. She didn't want to see him, didn't want to sleep in the same room with him or wonder if he was correct about to some of those observations he'd had no right to make.

How could he presume to know more about her family than she did? Lily didn't care if her mother had adored him, her brothers had trusted him with the secret shenanigans of their teen years and she—No, she refused to think about that now.

She was too angry to admit that she still carried feelings for him, so heavy sometimes that she worried they would crush her. She certainly didn't want him to know that now.

Once inside her room, she stripped off her clothes and pulled on the same pajamas she'd worn the previous day. As she slid beneath the sheets, her gaze came to rest on the blanket folded at the bottom of the bed. The one he'd stretched over her the night before. She didn't want to think about that, either.

She flipped off the lamp, leaving only the nightlight on so he wouldn't break his neck when he came into the room.

Earlier, she'd wondered if she would be able to sleep when she could think of nothing but how perfectly she'd still fit in his arms and how automatically he'd closed them around her. As if he wasn't as over her as he'd claimed. But now she wanted to get him out of her mind. If she couldn't do that, at least she could shut him out of her sight. She squeezed her eyes shut and waited for what felt like a long time to fall into a frustrated sleep.

Chapter 8

"WAKE UP, SUNSHINE," C.J. called out as the bedroom door burst open just as it had the day before.

Only this time the intruder was the same actor cast in the dream from which she'd just been torn. She was as confused by the dream as she was by his crash entry that morning. Shouldn't he already have been inside the room?

"Get up. We have a lot of work to do today."

Lily blinked as C.J. flipped the switch since there was no light coming in through the blind slats yet.

"But I just went to bed," she whined.

"Nope, it's been a whole night." He glanced at the digital numbers on the clock at her bedside. "Well, almost a night."

She rubbed at her eyes. "Why are you so chipper? You went to bed after I did."

"Well..."

She followed his gaze to the trundle bed. Like the previous day, it was neatly made with a blanket folded at its foot. Either he'd been a stealthy bed ninja and had sneaked by her twice without waking her, or he hadn't spent the night in that room.

"Where did you sleep?"

"Sleep?" He tilted his head one way and then the other to stretch his neck. "Not much of that, but I *rested* on the living

43

room sofa. Phil was right. That was like trying to nap on a stack of bricks."

"Why did you do it?" She indicated with a shift of her head the empty bed across the room.

He grinned. "I figured I was *persona non grata* in here last night."

"I wouldn't have forced you to sleep on the couch. Can you imagine the heat my brothers would have given me if I had?"

"Wish I'd known you felt that way. I'll be the one mainlining coffee today."

She would be guzzling java, too, but there was no way she would tell him why. Though she'd slept more than he had, hers had been a fitful sleep, too full of dreams for her to get any rest. He'd played a role in every one.

"Now you're up, right? You won't go back to sleep as soon as I close this door, will you?"

She'd just been throwing back the covers, but at his words, she stopped and looked toward the doorway again. She'd spoken almost the exact words to him that day so long ago. She'd been leaving for class at the time, and she'd returned to find him still asleep in her Lansing apartment when he should have been back at the Howell restaurant he worked in, prepping for the lunch rush. He'd lied then, letting her believe that his calling off at the last minute wouldn't affect his possible promotion. He'd even coaxed her back to bed and had distracted her with pleasure while he'd damaged his career to be with her.

Now as C.J. stared at her, she realized that if he was recalling the same conversation, he wasn't remembering it with the same remorse she was experiencing. His gaze was so direct that she felt held in place by it. So warm she expected her hair to catch on fire. Other parts of her were toasty enough to roast a marshmallow or two.

His gaze dipped from her face to the strappy sleep top that she hadn't thought to cover this time. Her cheeks burned. It was already too late to hide that her breasts had responded to nothing more than a look from him, but she tried anyway. At least he couldn't see all the bending and stretching taking place beneath her pajama bottoms. A gal had to keep at least a shred of her dignity.

"You'll be downstairs soon?"

A small smile played on his lips as he asked. If she'd believed he'd missed the signs of her body's response to him, she gave up on that fallacy.

"Yeah. Soon." As soon as her temperature returned to normal, and she could breathe again.

He took pity on her and stepped out of the room, closing the door behind him.

Lily could only stare at the door. Well, she wouldn't be going back to sleep anyway. She yanked off her pajamas and dressed in jeans, a roomy, long-sleeved T-shirt and tennis shoes. It didn't matter what she wore now. She couldn't cover what C.J. had already seen.

How was she supposed to face him now that he knew he could still strum her body like an acoustic guitar without ever touching the strings? There was nothing she could do to hide that truth. Why had she even tried? He was a man of the world now. He'd probably been able to read her response to him from the moment he'd met her at the airport. He probably knew all the ways to touch *any* woman to make her purr and call his name. The things he'd always been able to do with her.

"You've got to stop," she whispered to her bedroom's walls.

She hurried to the bathroom, splashed water on her face and then stared at the damp-skinned woman in the mirror. The woman who needed to get her priorities straight.

Of course, being near C.J. again had revived old memories and stirred up old feelings, but she couldn't forget why they were there in the first place. This was for Mom. This meal was Lily's atonement for opportunities missed, and she couldn't blow this chance to make things right, if only in her own heart. If that meant working alongside a man who made her skin tingle from nothing more than his nearness, then she would do that, too.

Her thoughts contained again, she brushed her teeth, tied back her hair and hurried downstairs to the kitchen.

She would make it through the next day-and-a-half if it required every bit of her determination and more acting skills than she'd ever displayed in an audition. Only later, when it was all over, would she worry about the cracks forming inside her heart.

Chapter 9

C.J. SENSED HER presence more than heard her as Lily walked into the kitchen no more than ten minutes after he'd returned downstairs. And after kicking off something he'd had no business starting.

Now when he should have been focused on recipes and a dish preparation schedule, all he could think about were her sleepy eyes, her curves outlined in that napkin of a top and how if she'd so much as nodded, he would have crawled right into that bed with her.

He had to get that idea, and her, out of his mind. Physical intimacy between them had never been the problem, anyway. Even though he hadn't been Mr. Experience, they'd mastered those mechanics from that first magical time. But sex was the easy part. The tough stuff involving hearts and trust were the things that one of them couldn't master.

"Glad you finally made it down here." He spoke over his shoulder, shifting around spice containers to look busy.

She cleared her throat. "What do you mean? I practically ran down here."

He only grunted. Would it be this awkward between them all day? They were there to cook dinner, and that was it. After sneaking a peek below his belt to ensure that she wouldn't be able to tell how much his body and his mind still disagreed on that subject, he slowly turned back to her.

"Let's get to work. Today we have pies, the cake, sweet-potato casserole—"

"How about we start with a little of that coffee you spoke of?" Lily said.

He gestured toward the full pot in the coffee maker. "Gotcha covered." He tightened his jaw. He refused to turn everything into innuendo the whole time they were working together.

"Thanks."

She grabbed a mug, poured some and, without adding cream, took a long pull on it. He knew she still hated to drink coffee that way, so she must have needed the caffeine boost.

"Prep cooks One and Two, reporting for duty."

Both Lily and C.J. turned to find Lily's sisters-in-law, Debbie and Tina, standing in the doorway, already wearing the aprons that had been hanging in the pantry earlier.

"Prep cooks?" Lily set her mug aside.

"Look," Debbie began with an uncertain smile, "we get how important it is for you to do this thing for your mom."

"Penny would have loved the gesture, by the way," Tina chimed in.

Debbie held her hands wide. "But you have to know that we loved your mom, too. Like she was our own mother. And we would like to be a part of this dinner to honor her. Even if it's in some minor way."

Tina grinned. "We've been checking out all of your fancy menus and place cards, and we want to get in on the action. How many times do you get the chance to see a real-life chef at work in a kitchen?"

Lily glanced back and forth between her sisters-in-law and C.J., seeming uncertain how to respond.

"Well, I'd say it's up to the chef of this meal." He pointed to Lily. "But even the best executive chefs need a staff. And these ladies have been looking up restaurant job titles online because prep cooks are just what you need. They can cut up all the vegetables for the veggie trays today and make the tossed salad tomorrow. They can even wash up dishes as we go along, if they're willing to do work outside their job descriptions."

Lily turned back to Debbie and Tina. "You're sure you have the time?"

Tina nodded. "The guys are in charge today and plan to take the kids on adventures. For us, it's a working vacation."

"And you don't mind doing the grunt work?"

This time, both of them nodded.

"Not as long as we get to watch the expert," Debbie said.

"And by that you mean watching Lily here, right?" C.J. pointed to her.

"Absolutely." Tina didn't even crack a smile.

Lily rolled her eyes. "Fine. But if you call me Chef Petunia or Chef Gladiola, like my brothers have probably instructed you to, I'll chase you out of the kitchen with a broom."

The other two women grinned as if they'd already been given some suggestions, but, again, they nodded.

Tina clapped her hands. "Sure glad that's settled because we had some things made at the embroidery store yesterday."

She backed out of the room and returned seconds later with a brown paper sack. From it, she withdrew two aprons, similar to the ones they wore. Only these two had "Chef Lily" and "Chef C.J." emblazoned on them.

Lily put her hand to her mouth, her eyes hot with tears. "Those are awesome. Thank you."

She hugged each of the women and allowed one of them to tie on her apron. When Debbie approached with his, C.J. turned around to let her tie it on him.

"I know you're used to wearing the fancy white coat," Debbie said.

"You kidding? I love this thing." He brushed his hands down the rough canvas material. "Thanks, ladies. It makes me feel like one of the family."

He blinked several times, grateful his voice hadn't cracked because of the lump that had formed in his throat. *Family.* Was that part of the annoyance he'd felt with Lily last night? She'd had the exact thing he craved, and she hadn't appreciated it back then. Maybe she still didn't.

He must have done a decent job at covering his weak moment because Tina was still grinning when she approached and patted his shoulder.

"Well, we're glad to have you, and not just because we're going to get to eat like queens on Thursday."

"Glad it's not just because of that."

He sneaked a peek at Lily and found her watching him, a curious expression on her face. Maybe he hadn't been as sly as he'd thought. Or maybe she just knew too much about his history and realized now she wasn't the only one with scars. But he couldn't afford to let her see too much. To let her get too close. She'd already proven what she would do with that kind of trust.

He looked away as he pulled his cellphone from his back pocket and clicked on the camera. "Here, can one of you two take a photo?"

Debbie took the phone from him as he scooted over to Lily, who looked as if she'd rather be doing anything than having her picture taken with him. He put his arm around her and tried to ignore that her shoulder tensed under his hand as he leaned in close. "Look, Chef Daisy, we're twins."

The comment earned him a frown from Lily and a photo that had to be retaken, but the joke was on him. He shouldn't have been that close and risked breathing in jasmine and peaches. He shouldn't have brushed the bottom of her ponytail and allowed the feel of silk to be imprinted on his fingertips. Didn't he understand that standing so close to the fire tended to singe more than eyebrows?

He carefully withdrew his hand and stepped forward to retrieve his phone and scroll through the half-dozen photos Debbie had taken.

"This one's my favorite." He flipped the phone so that Lily could see her frowning face.

"If you post that one, I'll track you down and beat you."

"Challenge accepted." He grinned at the other women this time instead of her. It was safer that way.

He gave Debbie and Tina instructions to make the veggie tray and then gathered the three small pie pumpkins he'd selected with Lily the day before.

"We need to get started on these." He set them on the counter in front of her.

She stared at them as if he'd just presented her with a bowl of live snails.

"I thought those were for decorations."

He shook his head. "No, these will be in the pumpkin pies."

"And what was wrong with the canned stuff?"

"Did you know that some cans of the pumpkin puree aren't even real pumpkin? They're a mixture of different types of squash."

"Oh, the shame of it!"

He gave her a dirty look. "You make fun of me now, but after you've made a homemade pie with the real pumpkin, you'll never be the same."

"And since this will be my first pie ever, I'm in for an even bigger change," she said with a chuckle. "I'm sensing a trend here. Canned, bad. Fresh, good."

"Not bad. Fresh is just better."

"And I'm about to spend my whole day under your tutelage to find out why," she said, an already tired smile on her lips.

Oh, he had some things he could teach her, all right. The thought struck him as if it had always been there, just waiting for him to notice it.

Maybe it was a good thing the other Monroe women would be sharing the kitchen with them this morning. Clearly, they needed chaperones. At least he did. Usually he was able to turn everything else off once he was inside the kitchen. It was his studio, where his function and necessity became art.

But today was different, no matter how much he tried to compartmentalize. No matter how many witnesses were there to keep him in check. He and Lily had started something today, and it was still simmering, just like his award-winning clam chowder, and it would take all of his strength to keep from going in for another taste.

Chapter 10

T Minus 18 Hours

HER HANDS COVERED with oven mitts, Lily pulled a cookie sheet with a pumpkin pie centered on it from the oven and set it on the stovetop. Then she leaned back in and lifted out the sheet containing the second pie.

She couldn't help staring down at her creations, their filling a deep orange, the fluted crust edges a perfect golden brown.

"They're amazing."

"Yes, they are." C.J. pulled out his phone and waited until she posed for a few photos. "You should be proud."

"And exhausted. I can't believe there are that many steps to bake a pie."

"Not any pie, but a…"

"*Real* pumpkin pie," she chimed along with him, having heard the same sing-songy ode to dessert for the past three hours. Baking and pureeing of the pumpkin flesh and then mixing the filling and rolling out the pie pastry had taken so long that they'd been able to mix, bake and even frost a Black Forest Cake with cherry filling in between steps.

At least staying busy had helped her keep her mind off that moment in her room earlier and what C.J. undoubtedly knew about her now. That she still wanted him. Had never stopped wanting him. But the intense way he'd looked back at her, did it mean he still wanted to be with her, too, even after everything?

"Do you want me to call the others back in so they can marvel over your accomplishments?" He indicated the doorway to the hall.

She shook her head. Her sisters-in-law had made it as long as they could before their kids demanded their attention, particularly Tina and Phil's eight-month-old, Lydia, who'd refused the bottle and cried for her mom instead.

"But don't you want them to see all your hard work?"

"That can wait until tomorrow." She gestured toward the cooling pies. "Anyway, my *work* would have gone a lot faster if we could have used the pie crust you rolled out on the counter next to mine. I wouldn't have had to make another one."

"That'd be cheatin'. You have to make the whole meal yourself."

"You wasted flour, salt *and* oil when you threw yours out."

"A necessary sacrifice," he said with a grin. "Emilio, our pastry chef at *Christopher's*, always says the only way to teach someone how to make pie crust is to have the student make his own right along with you."

"You mean to tell me you're not even the expert on this stuff, and you're trying to teach it to *me*?"

"Why do you think I had you make a simple cake and the pies instead of something hard like Chocolate *Soufflé*?" He chuckled as he reached for the cake carrier and tested its edges to make sure it was sealed. "I get by with the dessert stuff anyway. In culinary school, we had to touch on several areas in addition to our specialization."

Lily had been joking before, but she suddenly turned serious. She'd been looking for a chance to explain a few things to him, and he'd given her an opening. "I'm glad you had the chance to follow your dream and go to culinary school."

"Yeah, me too. Though I'm still paying on those loans from Johnson & Wales."

"Well, you did attend a world-renowned program."

"Been studying them?"

He was kidding her again about researching him, and she could have dropped the subject, but she needed him to know the truth about why she'd let him go.

"I worried that you wouldn't go through with it. Culinary school, you know." It was easier to say these things if she didn't look at him, so she carefully lifted one of the pies from the cookie sheet and placed it on the cooling rack.

"Worried?"

She could feel the intensity of his stare on her back, but she couldn't turn his way. Would her feelings be right there for him to see? For him to reject?

"Oh, you mean after you destroyed me?"

She couldn't help it. She flinched. His words stung worse than a slap. If only she could tell him that she'd done it all for him. If only he would believe her if she did.

But when Lily glanced back at him over her shoulder, C.J. didn't look at her.

"It's over," he said. "I survived. I even had a lot of extra time to learn to make *portefeuilles* or *estouffades*, so I should say thank you." He cleared his throat. "Thank you."

"It's not funny."

His making light of it with his fancy French cooking terms only made her wonder if she'd hurt him more than he wanted to let on? He wouldn't look at her, so she couldn't read his expression. Had he felt as lost as she had? Was there a possibility that even though he'd approached moving on to other women like an Olympic athlete chasing gold that he'd really been fleeing from his own pain?

She hated that she'd hurt him, but she reassured herself that his pain had been only temporary. Not like the recurring sorrow she would have caused him if she'd deprived him of his dream. For that, she never would have forgiven herself.

"Well, I'm happy for you. For everything you've accomplished. I always wanted good things for you. All good things."

"As long as you weren't one of them."

She shook her head. "That's not how it was."

"Then how was it?"

He pinned her with his stare, and she couldn't help but squirm. Suddenly, the explanation she'd longed to give him seemed woefully inadequate. She'd always worried he wouldn't believe her if she told him the truth. Now she was too nervous to find out if she was right.

Instead of answering, she gestured toward the countertops, still covered with boxes and canisters. "Shouldn't we be getting something else done? Thanksgiving's tomorrow."

He studied her for several seconds and then shrugged. Since she was the one who'd brought up the past, she was grateful he didn't say so. She would tell him the truth eventually, just not now.

"Well, let's see what's left." C.J. ticked off items on his fingers. "The dough for the yeast rolls is in the refrigerator. The sweet potato casserole is there, too, ready to go in the oven. We've even baked the cornbread to go in the stuffing."

"Anything else?" She couldn't help pressing. She was a bundle of nervous energy, and she needed something to keep her hands busy.

"Aren't you tired?" he asked. "I know I am."

Lily gestured again at the many unopened packages. "But there still has to be a lot to do. What is Dad going to think when we have to feed everyone dessert and nothing else because we didn't get dinner finished?"

"Classic chef anxiety."

"What are you talking about?"

"You're just getting nervous. Look, you've done a wonderful job today, and you'll do great tomorrow. I'll be there, and Tina and Debbie will help us get the whole thing on the table." He nodded as if to confirm his own words. "You're going to rock this."

"I sure hope so." In the past few days she'd come to hope a lot of things that had nothing to do with making a holiday dinner. Things she had no business hoping. Instead of admitting that, she stepped over to the sink and rinsed the last few dishes. Anything to stay busy.

"And, Lily…"

She looked over her shoulder at him.

"I'm proud of you." He smiled. "Your mom would be, too."

Lily's breath caught. Guilt pressed down on her shoulders like a lead blanket, its poison spilling into her bloodstream. How could he be proud of her, let alone believe her mother would be, when Lily had forgotten so many times these past three days why she was there in the first place? When even her too-little-too-late gesture had been a selfish one, to relieve her own shame.

She trembled with the knowledge that she was that selfish person she'd sworn never to become. The one who only thought of herself. She was just like her mother, after all.

Chapter 11

T Minus 16 Hours

LILY WAS STILL shaking when she climbed into bed and pulled the covers up to her chin. She'd taken extra time washing her face in the hall bathroom, hoping C.J. would already be asleep when she slipped into her bedroom. His slow, steady breathing now suggested she'd guessed right.

She exhaled slowly and pulled the blankets up over her head until she'd made a cocoon for herself. She couldn't talk to him now, couldn't tell him what an awful daughter and person she was, couldn't reinforce for him that he'd always been better off without her. Only when she was as alone as she could be in a house stuffed with people did she finally acquiesce to the heat building behind her eyes and the humiliation crowding her heart.

She turned and buried her face in the pillow to mask any sounds. Her tears dampened the sheet and the blanket touching her face, but she didn't care. She deserved this. Someone like her deserved to be alone.

She startled as something settled on the mattress next to her. A familiar hand gently squeezed her shoulder.

"What's going on, Lil?"

He pulled the blanket back before she could tighten it over her.

"Nothing." She turned her head to the side but didn't try to lift it off the pillow. "I...thought you were...asleep. I'm...fine."

"Not *nothing*. I wasn't asleep. And you're not close to fine." As he spoke, he drew soothing circles on her back, drying her tears in a way she hadn't been able to do herself.

"Now sit up here and talk to me."

She shook her head but found herself following his instructions. As soon as she flipped over, C.J. gathered her to him, resting her cheek against his shoulder. Where the room had seemed claustrophobic with the two of them together in the daylight, she felt safe now in his arms.

"Talk," he repeated softly.

"Mom wouldn't be proud...of me. You shouldn't be, either. No one should." She stopped as sobs racked her chest again.

"Of course, we should."

She refused to accept his words. "I'm a liar. I'm weak. I'm selfish."

"I don't think you're any of those things. You're a good person. You're smart. You're funny. You're sensitive."

His breathing was calm and so comforting that she wanted to believe him, but she knew the truth, and she needed to tell him as well.

"No one knows it, but I'm a...bust...in L.A."

"You and ninety-nine percent of your fellow working actors."

Strange that he didn't sound surprised, but she couldn't let him make excuses for her. "Even the dinner we're cooking. I'm only here because I feel guilty that I never fixed things with Mom. And even then, I couldn't make it about her. Instead I had to make about—"

She stopped herself and stilled against his chest.

"About what?"

His voice was a hoarse whisper.

For several seconds, she held her breath, her world spinning too quickly and no opportunity to exit the ride. He rested his hands on her shoulders and carefully drew her away from him.

"About what?" he asked again, this time his voice gentle.

In darkness too deep for her to see more than his shadowed outline, she sensed his gaze on her face. Steady. Unrelenting.

"Us."

Her word came as quietly as a breath, but she knew he'd heard her as his fingertips tightened against her skin.

For a second, or ten thousand, neither moved, the only sounds coming from their mingling breaths, no longer as calm as before.

When Lily was certain she would lose her mind if he didn't say something, C.J. bent his head and pressed his lips to her forehead. Nothing could have stopped her from leaning into the sweetness and security she'd only ever known with him.

As he shifted back, she leaned in to follow his retreat, but he only slid over to kiss her eyebrows by turns and then her eyelids. By the time that his lips moved to her cheekbone and then the side of her face, so close to the corner of her mouth, Lily was convinced that she would die from anticipation of what would come next. What *had to* come next.

And then it did. He brushed his lips over hers, once, twice, three times, and then covered her mouth with a kiss so intense she stretched toward him to get a better taste. His kiss was different now due to the slight roughness of his beard and years of honing his skills. Yet it was familiar as well. Like coming home to the only place she'd ever truly belonged.

When he slanted his mouth over hers and traced his tongue along the seam of her lips, she welcomed him with an urgency that made him catch his breath. She wasn't sure when her hands had released their grip on the covers to shift to the wide planes of his back, but there they were, his muscles flexing beneath her touch.

As his fingertips glided from her shoulders and skimmed the sides of breasts that were already straining against her tank top, Lily's eyes flew open, and she turned her head to the side.

"This is a bad idea." Even as she whispered it, her hands seemed to have a plan of their own and slid down his sides, her thumbs coming to rest on his pelvic bones. "You'll be sorry. I'll be sorry."

C.J. dipped his head and traced a line of kisses on the side of her neck, lingering on a sensitive spot just behind her ear. The one he hadn't forgotten, even after all the other women. She shivered just as she always had under the magic of his touch.

"I'll never be sorry," he breathed against her skin.

If only she could believe him. And if only she could say the same. Could she risk giving herself over to this wave of passion threatening to capture her in its undertow? C.J. had changed. He wasn't the same guy she'd walked away from for his own good. He didn't even believe in forever now. Would she be the one he left behind this time after she let him touch her body or, so much worse, her heart?

"Still considering?"

His whispered words blazed a trail along the side of her neck that his lips followed, and his skilled hands started off on their own adventure over curves and planes and tender places. With each feather of a touch, she both lost and won.

"Maybe we should…" She would have said *stop*, but the lie about what she wanted refused to form on her lips.

"Let me love you, Lil. Just this once," he crooned even as he guided her back onto the pillow and leaned in close above her.

Once? The word echoed inside her head, stark in its finality.

But it was the other word she gathered close to her heart as she pushed the covers further back and reached out to pull him under them. *Love.* It meant everything and nothing, but right now it was all she had. All she could hope for.

"I need you to say it, sweetheart," he said in a low, strained grumble. "I need to know you want this."

"I want...you." She paused, her face burning with humiliation. "Please."

She stared at his form in the darkness and waited, only their ragged breaths disturbing the stillness. Then C.J. made a sound like a groan deep in his throat.

"I've missed this," he whispered. Even quieter, he added, "I've missed *us.*"

When C.J. covered her mouth with his again, there was no finesse to his movement, only desire, stark and unrepentant. Lily lifted up on the bed to climb more fully into his kiss, her need for him stronger than anything she'd ever experienced. Tomorrow couldn't matter. Only now. Only this.

As clothing slipped away, piece by piece, Lily reveled in the touches and tastes and textures that had always been theirs. But they were different now, better, as if perfected by distance and time. She gave herself to him with desperation for every moment they'd missed and for every second they would never have.

She drifted off to sleep in his arms, praying that tomorrow would never come.

Chapter 12

T Minus 9 Hours

C.J. KNEW HE was a cliché, but he was practically whistling as he headed into the kitchen, even though he'd had just a few hours of sleep. He brushed his hand back through his hair, still damp from a shower, and traced his thumb and forefinger over his freshly-trimmed beard. He should have used his scissors *before* he'd gone to bed so he wouldn't have abraded her skin, but he hadn't known that such an amazing night was in store for them.

The kitchen was still dark, which was a good thing. At least he had a few more minutes to prepare himself before seeing Lily this morning. He wasn't sure he would be able to keep his hands off her when he did. Not that he'd actually *seen* her last night, even if her soft skin, silky hair and the delicate rises and falls of her curves were forever imprinted on his fingertips. And his heart.

He'd always told himself that his memory had exaggerated the awesomeness of loving Lily Monroe, like an older child recalling the death-defying hills of the kiddie roller coaster. But his recollections had been breathtakingly accurate. Her scent. Her taste. Her essence. She might not have been the only woman he'd ever touched, but she was the only one who touched *him* and left her mark much deeper than on his skin.

For him, Lily had always been *it*. And she'd begged him last night. He hoped that meant something. He'd longed to hear her tell him she loved him the way she used to, but then he hadn't spoken those words, either. Their rekindled relationship was still too new, its beginning still fragile.

To keep busy, he started a huge pot of coffee for when all the family members started trickling in and filling their mugs. His hands itched to get started on dinner, but he had to wait for her so that she could do the work. This was Lily's big day, and he didn't want to take that from her.

"Oh. I didn't expect anyone to be in here yet."

At the doorway, she stood chewing her bottom lip, as if deciding whether or not to enter the room. Something tightened inside C.J.'s gut, but he pushed the feeling aside.

"I saw that you were already up, and I heard the shower down the hall. I got ready in the downstairs bathroom," he said.

Instead of mentioning how disappointed he'd been to wake up alone in her tiny bed, he gave her a tired smile. "I didn't think we'd be getting to work so early, especially after—"

"I just wanted to get started," she said. "We still have so many things to do. We're running out of time."

Why did he feel as if the possibilities between them were running out as well? Lily couldn't even let him say aloud what had happened between them. The unsettled feeling inside him squeezed tighter. He supposed he should have expected some morning-after awkwardness between them, even if, like Phil had said, it wasn't the first time. Or was it something more than that? He'd said *just this once*. He hoped she understood he hadn't meant it.

"There's still plenty of time, you know," he said to fill the awkward silence. "Dinner's not until three."

"Well, some of us don't make elaborate dinners every day of our lives. Or any dinners." She blew out a breath and tromped past him to the coffee maker. "I just want to get it right. For Mom."

But her actions didn't seem to have anything to do with the dinner or her mother. She couldn't even look at him, and her hand was so unsteady that as she poured, a ring of spilled coffee formed around the outside of her mug.

"We should talk about what happened last night," he said.

She shook her head so hard that coffee sloshed over the cup's rim, burning her hand, but she barely flinched. "Look, there's nothing to talk about. It doesn't have to change anything. It was probably a mistake—"

"Mistake?" The word came out before he could stop it, sharper and more revealing than he'd hoped. Anxiety transformed into acrimony in the time it took to cross from the sink to the counter where she stood. "You were there. How can you say it was a mistake?"

He wished he could play it off as a one-night stand, but it never had been. At least not to him.

Instead of backing away, she set her coffee aside and crossed her arms. "You know I'm right."

"Do I?" The uncertainty in her eyes only emboldened him. "I don't think you believe that."

She shook her head. "I can't...be with you."

"Can't? Or won't?"

"I don't know." She closed her eyes, shaking her head again. "Both."

C.J. would have said more—Lily definitely deserved to *hear* more—but a sound behind him had him turning back to the door. Debbie and Tina, both dressed in sweats and looking as if they'd just rolled out of bed, padded into the kitchen. He glanced at Lily to let her know that their conversation wasn't over, but she wouldn't look at him.

"Where's the coffee?" Even as Tina asked the question, she

hurried across the room and lunged for the coffee pot. She filled two mugs and handed one to her grateful partner.

"Sorry you volunteered to help?" C.J. tried to keep his voice light. It was the best he could do.

Debbie took a long drink and then shook her head. "We were dying to get up at the crack of dawn to *not* cook with you."

He stepped to the refrigerator and stuck his head inside, not even sure what he was looking for. The others might be mildly sorry to be there, but his list of regrets was longer. What had he been thinking, climbing into her bed again, much less telling himself it might mean something? Worse than that, he still had to cook with her today. Even if he hadn't been smart enough to stay away from her for his self-preservation, he knew better than to get involved with a fellow worker in the kitchen. At least in *his* kitchen.

Now he had to live with his mistake. No matter how awkward it would be with Lily, especially with witnesses, he would somehow help her to make an edible Thanksgiving dinner, just as he'd promised. But if she thought she was going to escape their conversation this morning just because they'd been interrupted, she had another think coming. He would have his say, and she was going to listen.

Chapter 13

Liftoff

LILY'S ARMS TREMBLED with strain as she carried the turkey on the huge white platter into the dining room. Ahead of her, two tables were covered with fancy linens, dishes that actually matched, autumn-themed centerpieces and some of the most beautiful creations she'd ever seen, let alone prepared.

She paused to admire the tables and the family members gathered around them, most wearing Sunday-best clothes they hated to match with the formal atmosphere and to be the subjects in C.J.'s photos.

"You sure you've got that?" he said from behind her.

"I've got it," she said, though she barely did.

Her stomach tightened as it had every time he'd spoken to her all day. Not that he'd said much other than to give her cooking instructions, and even those words had come with a growl. Obviously, he was angry over what she'd said about last night, but he had to understand how confused she was. If only he could see how hard this was for her, how much she wished she could forget the commitment she'd made to herself and could hide with him under the covers all day.

She couldn't imagine how her sisters-in-law had missed the tension between them, taut as a tightrope stretched across the kitchen. Yet even with the extra stress she could have blamed if any of the food had boiled over or caught fire, she was amazed to see that every dish had turned out perfectly. All of them.

At least when he came up behind her and spoke this time, she'd managed not to jump, or the turkey would have done a triple flip onto the floor.

Garrett waved with his carving knife from his place at the head of the table. "Well, get that bird over here. We're starving, and I still need to show off my carving skills."

"Yeah, I was considering eating the stuff in those flower pots," Peter announced from the other end of the table, where he was seated between Debbie and Evan. "Do you think they're edible?"

From his chair next to their father, Phil waved the piece of parchment that had been resting on his plate in front of the turkey napkin. "I don't know what this is, but I was thinking of eating it, too."

Across from him, bouncing baby Lydia on her knee, Tina frowned. "Your menu? I married a man with no class."

"Hey, I'm classy. My fancy name card is right here."

Tina shook her head. "Place cards, and we all have them."

They all showed their cards then, even the four children at the kids' table.

"It's not fair, Dad," eight-year-old Michael announced. "Why do I have to sit with the kids?"

"Because you're a kid, that's why," Peter informed his second son.

Evan grinned at his brother from his spot at the adult table. "Yeah. You're a kid."

Garrett led the family in grace and sliced a selection of drum sticks and light and dark meat. Then they all started passing dishes, laughing and eating.

Everyone, that is, except C.J.

Lily sensed his gaze on her, but every time she peeked over

at him, he was poking at his turkey or studying the cornbread stuffing she'd made with sausage and fennel. He wasn't even taking as many photos as he probably needed for his blog.

Though she was too stressed to be hungry now, she took a spoonful from each dish and sampled them all. The turkey was moist, and each side dish tasted as good as it looked. The murmurs of enjoyment around her told that the rest of her family agreed.

"This dinner is amazing, sweetheart." Garrett raised his wine glass in a salute to his daughter and her cooking skills.

"Yeah, you done good, Begonia." Peter gestured at the many dishes on the table.

"He's right, Buttercup," Phil agreed.

"Thanks, guys, but one of these days you're going to run out of flower names," she said.

"Never!" The twins declared in unison.

"Roy's going to eat like a king dog tonight," Evan announced.

Garrett scanned the table again. "Your mom would be proud of you."

The emotion that swirled in and clogged Lily's throat surprised her, but it shouldn't have. This was the dinner she'd planned. The gift she'd longed to give. With a lot of help from C.J. and the others, she'd even pulled it off. She reached beneath her and smoothed a hand over the sturdy wood chair her mother used to sit on.

This one's for you, Mom.

Strange, but during the past few days this dinner had become more than a symbol of the debt she owed. It had come to represent what she wanted, too. And she wanted *this*. She needed to know the people around this table, to be invested in their lives. She needed the man seated to her left as well, the one it hurt her heart to look at and her fingers ached to touch, but she couldn't think about that now. Sometimes people weren't meant to have everything they wanted.

"I miss Grandma," four-year-old Sidney announced.

Silence fell around both tables as everyone set their forks aside and took a moment to miss her together.

Garrett cleared his throat to signal an end to the moment of silence and then pointed to C.J. "Thank you for showing my daughter all your magic."

When the twins sniggered like the sophomores they'd never ceased to be, their father frowned at them. "I mean in the kitchen."

Though both of his sons waggled their eyebrows in nearly identical expressions, Garrett ignored them this time.

"It was all her," C.J. said to end the awkward silence. He gestured toward Lily in the chair next to him, but he didn't look at her as he spoke.

"She made everything. The cranberry sauce. The roasted square potatoes with bay leaves. Just wait until you taste the pumpkin pies with real whipped cream and the Black Forest cake."

"She definitely did it all," Tina piped from the other end of the table.

"And did you get one of her yeast rolls—" C.J. stopped himself and shot a look down the table. "Where are—"

"Hey, Mommy," the kindergartner, Avery, called out from the kids' table. "What's that smell?"

"Is something burning?" six-year-old Troy wanted to know.

"The yeast rolls!" Lily squealed.

Evan and Michael beat everyone else in a race to the kitchen. Evan returned a minute later wearing oven mitts and carrying two cookie sheets covered with charred lumps.

"Maybe don't try the yeast rolls," Peter said.

They all laughed. Except C.J.

"It wouldn't have been a meal if I hadn't burned something," Lily said.

C.J. stirred the cranberry sauce around on his plate. "Those rolls wouldn't have burned, either, if you'd set the timer on the oven like I told you to."

"Sorry. Everything just got hectic, and I—"

"Didn't bother to set the timer," he finished for her. "I had to call in my lifetime supply of favors just to get people to cover for me at the restaurant during Thanksgiving week, and all I asked was that you follow my instructions. You couldn't even do that much."

Lily couldn't help staring at him. "Now hold on a minute. I did *everything* you told me to do in that kitchen. For three days."

"Apparently not everything."

"Well, almost everything. I stirred. I cubed stuff. I stuck my hand in a turkey's butt."

Ever helpful Phil pointed out, "Well, technically, the hole is at the top of its body, where its head used to be."

"Ew," the two little girls chorused.

"But you didn't set the timer," C.J. pressed.

Lily caught the others trading curious looks, but she didn't care. She glared at him, even if he didn't have the guts to look back at her. "No. I didn't set the timer. I burned your perfect rolls."

"It's not just that," he said as he finally looked up at her.

Garrett tapped his spoon on the side of his glass. "What the hell is going on with you two?"

Lily vaguely heard her father, but she couldn't answer him, not until she'd said everything she need to say.

"And, once again, if you treat the people who work for you half as badly as you've treated me, I predict you won't have any

71

employees at all by Christmas."

"You're one to talk to me about how I treat people. Not with the way you do it."

"What do you mean by that?"

"I just thought things were different after last night—"

Lily recognized the absolute second that C.J. realized he'd gone too far because he halted his words. She gasped. Her face burned all the way to her scalp.

"I knew it!" Debbie called out.

"Who couldn't have figured out what happened in that bedroom last night?" Peter agreed with his wife. Since C.J. was seated across from him, he offered his friend an air high-five, but C.J. only tightened his jaw and stared down at his plate.

All around the adult table, everyone nodded their agreement. Even Evan, who understood too much for his own good.

"There was such a slow burn in that kitchen today that I thought the whole room would go up in flames," Tina said with a chuckle. "Not just the rolls."

Lily swallowed. Her sisters-in-law hadn't been oblivious after all.

Her father pushed back from the table, but just when Lily thought he might come to her rescue, he added a comment.

"Guess that room was a little too cozy."

She gave her relatives dirty looks by turns.

"I'm glad to be entertainment for everyone, but I don't need this." She pushed back from the table and stood.

"Wait, Lily."

She started toward the door but turned back at C.J.'s words. "What do you want?"

"You can't walk away from this." He stood next to her and rested his hand on her arm. "Not this time."

Chapter 14

T Plus 45 Minutes

INSTEAD SHE RAN.

Lily shook away his hold on her arm and rushed from the room. She couldn't decide whether she was more embarrassed or furious. At her family for feeding into her humiliation. At C.J. for talking to her that way. And for asking questions she couldn't answer.

She didn't care if he followed her or not. She rushed into the State Police room and slammed the door. As she slumped into her mother's executive chair, she tried to ignore the irony of that location. There'd been plenty of door-slamming in her relationship with her mom.

Heavy footfalls announced C.J.'s approach. He didn't bother knocking before pushing the door open.

"I told you…you can't walk away. Not again."

Lily had to unclench her jaw before she could even speak. "That is what you came here to say after you've just told my whole family, including my nieces and nephews, about my sex life…at Thanksgiving dinner?"

He scooted the guest chair up to the desk and dropped into it. "Sorry. That wasn't my most shining moment. And my timing stank. But that doesn't mean that it's okay for you to walk away, *again*, without giving me a real explanation. I deserve at least that much."

"You've been playing the field for years, *Christopher*." She paused as his eyes narrowed over her use of his full name as his playboy alter ego. "You should know what a one-night stand looks like."

Hurt flashed in his eyes, but he quickly masked it. "That's the story you're going to stick with? Because what happened between us last night wasn't like any hookup I can remember."

Lily couldn't look at him. She had no experience with casual sex, yet she was positive no one-nighter could come close to comparing to that tender evening they'd shared.

"Tell me the truth. About then and now. I can take it."

"Even if it means I have to tell you that I just don't want you?" She stared at her hands now, wondering why she bothered to tell that lie when it obviously was one. She shook her head. "You don't know what you're asking for. You'll never understand."

"Tell me, anyway. You owe me that much."

"Do I? After I did it all for you? Then and now."

The words came out in a rush, which was only right for a truth held so long and so closely to her heart. Relief lifted the weight she'd carried.

For several seconds, he seemed to chew on her comment and digest it. Then he trapped her with his stare.

"Now let me get this straight. I asked you to marry me, and as your answer, you broke up with me. After that, you ran away to L.A. and an acting career. And now you're saying you did it all for *me*?"

It sounded ridiculous when he put it that way, but she tried to explain anyway.

"Well, maybe not the L.A. part, but it's still connected. Look, I tried to tell you this the other night." She held her hands wide to indicate the memorabilia from her mother's law-enforcement career. "I couldn't let you give up your dreams to help me pursue mine. Like Dad did for Mom."

"We're back to that again?"

She shook her head. "You didn't get it the first time I tried to explain."

"You say you walked away from me for my own good. Like you were some self-sacrificing Florence Nightingale." He planted his hands on the edge of the desk. "Well, I call bullshit."

"You're telling me you still would have gone to culinary school if we'd stayed together? That you wouldn't have decided it wasn't necessary?"

"I'd like to think I would have made the decision *with* you, but we'll never know, will we?"

He studied her for so long that she shifted under his accusing stare.

"And then you say you did it for my own good."

"You see." She waved a hand toward him. "This is why I never told you. I knew you wouldn't believe me."

"Because you were lying. To yourself and to me."

"I wasn't...I'm *not*...lying." She crossed her arms in a tight hug, as if that could shield her from his words.

"Then where does the guy fit into your philanthropic decision? Was it Tim or Tom? You know, the one you were madly in love with."

"Brad." She lifted her shoulder and lowered it. "He was just a means to an end. I only went out with him twice."

She held her hands wide in a plea for understanding. "I had to tell you something you would believe, or you would have tried to talk me out of it."

"You mean...you *lied*?"

"For you? A little white one."

"That nearly shredded my heart."

She swallowed now. He'd never admitted before just how much she'd hurt him, and his words threw acid on a thinly-scarred wound. "I'm sorry for any pain I've caused you, but I look at how successful you've become, and I'm so proud of you. I'll never be sorry for that."

"And you did it all for *me*."

He used both hands to shove his chair back from the table so hard it tipped backward. When the front legs thumped to the floor again, he leaped up from the seat and started pacing. As he stood before a portrait taken the day of her mother's promotion to lieutenant, he spoke to Lily over his shoulder.

"You do belong in Hollywood." He shook his head, smiling though his words were anything but happy. "You've lied to yourself for so long, and you're so good at it, that even you can no longer tell what the truth is."

She settled her elbows on the desk and gripped her head in her hands. "You don't know what it's like to love someone so much you're convinced your heart will bleed if you lose him. But you leave him anyway because you know you're selfish, and you're terrified you'll hurt him when you turn out just like your mother."

He stopped pacing and stared her down. "This isn't about your mom. It never was. You felt crazy and out of control when you were with me, and those feelings scared the hell out of you. I know what that's like because loving you felt that way to me, too. But I'm not the one who ran. You did."

"You've got it all wrong. Don't you see that? I want you. I've always wanted you. And I love you. Didn't last night at least show you that?"

He paused for a few seconds and watched her, his expression softening, as though she'd finally gotten through to him. But then his jaw tightened again.

"All that proves is you don't have the courage to fight for

what you want."

She could only shake her head.

"And if everything you've said is true," he continued, "then I have one question to you ask you."

She met his gaze warily. "What's that?"

"Why not now? If you gave me my freedom to protect me from abandoning my dreams for you, then shouldn't now be the perfect time? I even have a restaurant with my name on it. I have my dream. Are you worried that I would throw it all away for you?"

"Of course not."

"Then I repeat, why not now?"

Lily opened her mouth to answer but found she had no words to say. Finally, she closed her lips and buried her face in her hands. She'd spent so long telling herself she was protecting him she'd never considered that those walls she'd constructed might have been to protect her own heart.

C.J. stepped closer to the door. "You always have to be the one to leave first, Lil, because that's easier than being left behind. I'm sorry, but that's not going to work out this time. You don't know how to trust, and I can't spend another six years waiting for you to figure out how. I'm done."

"Please don't leave like this. We can talk about it."

"And say what?" He paused, but when she wasn't fast enough to fill in the blank, he added, "I've always known what I wanted. Too bad you could never figure it out."

She searched madly, but the words wouldn't come. It had taken her too long to realize that it was fear keeping her from having what she wanted. And now she'd lost him.

Just as his hand closed over the doorknob, a knock came from the other side.

Phil pushed open the door and leaned inside. "Sorry, C.J. Sorry, Lil. I know you're busy, but we were getting ready to cut the pies, and since you made them, we hoped you would be there."

Beneath Phil's elbow, Avery leaned her blond head inside. "Who wants pie?"

Lily shook her head. "You guys go ahead."

But C.J. opened the door wide.

"Sure, I'll take some pie," he told Avery, who ran ahead of the adults.

He lowered his voice, but it was still loud enough for Lily to hear. "I'll be taking mine to go."

Chapter 15

LILY JERKED AT the sound of someone knocking. She blinked several times and glanced around the room, where the furniture, photos and books had become shadows. What had happened to the daylight? Just how long had she been sitting there beating herself up? Not long enough, as far as she was concerned. Her eyes burned, but she refused to let herself cry anymore. C.J. was gone, and she had no one to blame but herself.

"Lily, honey," her father called from outside the door. "You okay?"

"I'm fine, Dad. I just need to be alone." Nothing could make a difference now, anyway. C.J. was right. All of her *sacrificing* to protect him had been about insulating her own heart from pain. But nothing could shield her from the emptiness she felt now as shame eclipsed all her fears.

Her father either couldn't hear her, or he chose not to listen as he opened the door and flipped the wall switch. Yellow light from the oversized lamp on the desk filled the room. Lily blinked several times as her eyes adjusted to the brightness.

"I thought I locked that door," she said.

Garrett opened his palm to show her the key. "It's my office, after all."

"Oh. Right."

Her gaze shifted around the room that she'd never thought of before as her father's office as well as her mother's.

"I just wanted to make sure you're all right. You've been in here a long time."

"Not that long."

But the wall clock read six o'clock. Lily pushed back her chair. She tried to stand, but her legs were tingly and ineffectual, so she leaned on the desk for balance.

"Oh, Dad. I'm sorry. I should have helped clean up dinner."

He waved away her apology. "Don't worry about it. The guys and I took clean-up duty. We put away the desserts, too. They were great. I tried the cake and the pie. We can get them back out again if you're hungry."

Lily dropped back into the chair and shook her head. She doubted she would ever be hungry again. "I really messed up this time."

Her father stepped over to the wall and took his time scanning her mother's recruit-class photo, though he could probably pick her out with his eyes closed. Front row, third from the left.

"Oh. How so?" he asked casually.

Lily almost smiled. This was the Dad she remembered, the parent who usually wielded his influence with flicks of a paintbrush rather than a whack over the head with a police baton. She realized now that those comparisons she'd made between her parents had always been unfair to her mother. Another mistake among many.

"He's gone, Dad." Her voice broke as she whispered the words. "I lost him."

"Yep, he left for the airport about as quickly as he could shove his clothes into his suitcase." He turned back from the photo. "Isn't that what you wanted?"

"No!"

"Then why did you send him away? Twice."

She lifted a brow. Her family wasn't supposed to know what had really happened in their breakup. But after C.J.'s comments at dinner, they all knew more than they had before. She lowered her head into her hands. "I don't know."

Garrett's chuckle made her look up again.

"Women." He shook his head. "The most precious creatures God ever put on this Earth. If only He'd sent an instruction guide along with them."

"You're not helping."

"Yeah, that's the thing about parenting. Sometimes you see the picture from a bigger lens since you've been around a lot longer, but you have to sit back and let your kids make their own mistakes and figure out how to live with them."

She laced fingers behind her crown and pulled down on it, letting her elbows fall close to her head. "I've made so many mistakes where C.J. is concerned. And about Mom."

"You and your mom were like oil and vinegar sometimes, but you need to know that she loved you fiercely. And she couldn't have been prouder of you for believing in yourself enough to take on Hollywood."

She lowered her arms. "Was she also proud that I've ended up flat on my face and have to wait tables just to feed myself?"

"She knew those things take time. We all knew." He smiled. "The cream always rises to the top."

"Or curdles. I never got to tell Mom...I was sorry." Again, her voice broke, a lifetime of regrets crammed into three powerful words.

"She knew. She felt the same."

For several seconds she watched him, needing from her core for his words to be true.

Garrett made a slow spin in the center of the office, seeming to take in the bookshelves, the photos, the memories.

"I think you've had a misconception all these years about how our family operated."

She shook her head to deny it, but her father raised a hand to hold her off.

"You seem to think that your mom forced me to give up my art to run this family so she could focus on her law-enforcement career." He rocked his head back and forth, as if considering her theory, and then crossed and sat in the same seat C.J. had occupied a few hours before. "Okay, maybe I put my painting in the backseat, but I made that decision. No one else."

He stared at her directly, seeming to dare her to contradict him. "These are things you need to know. I love my life. I *chose* my life. And I'm as proud of my decisions as I was of...my wife."

His voice faltered as he pointed to her portrait on the wall. He cleared his throat. "I'm proud that we were—and are—a Michigan State Police family."

"I'm proud, too," she said in a small voice.

"Really?"

"Yes. Really." She smiled as she realized it was true.

"But I don't think we're here to discuss my decisions, are we?"

"I have to figure out what to do."

"I think you already know."

Did she? Was she prepared to lay her heart on the line for C.J. when he could trample all over it? What if she finally showed she had the courage to fight for what she wanted, and she lost him anyway?

"The way I look at it, there are two questions you need to ask yourself."

Since she had more than just two, she lifted her head and waited.

"One, do you love him? Two, do you want to be with him?"

Lily swallowed. Even with all the uncertainties swirling in her thoughts, it really was just that simple. "Yes and yes."

"Then what are you doing here with me?"

"You're right. What am I doing here?" She pushed the chair further from the desk, stood and hurried from the room.

She was halfway up the stairs, making plans with each step, but then she stopped and turned back. Her father stood at the foot of the steps, looking up.

"I'm going to need a ride to the airport in about ten minutes, okay?"

He nodded. "I'll warm up the car."

"And Dad?"

He'd taken a step toward the garage, but Garrett stopped and glanced back.

"Could you pack me some pie as well?" She smiled. "I need to keep up my strength for this."

Chapter 16

T plus 4 hours 15 minutes

C.J. GLANCED UP from the boarding pass resting on his lap just as the airline gate agent made the first announcement for pre-boarding in first-class. He still had some time since the seat he'd finally managed to get, for far more than he should have had to pay, was in chattel class. But, on the other hand, he would have paid any price to get back to Boston today.

He didn't bother telling himself he shouldn't have come at all. His heart might have more lacerations than even before, but maybe after they healed a little, he would really be able to let Lily go. And not just tell himself he was doing it.

Taking a deep breath, he stood, stuffed his boarding pass in his jacket pocket and hoisted his laptop bag onto his shoulder. He grabbed the handle of his carry-on and pulled it behind him. Unless the plane was delayed once they were on the tarmac, he would make it back to *Christopher's* before midnight and might be able to get some bills paid before sunrise. He sidled over to the cluster of travelers who were pretending to form a single line to the open boarding door.

"C.J., wait!"

He froze, his pulse pounding so loudly in his ears that the conversations of the other holiday travelers were muted around him. Slowly, he turned toward her, just as Lily stopped right in front of him, out of breath from running. She looked as tired and worn as he felt, and her face was puffy, as if she'd been crying.

"What are you doing here?" He'd hoped he could speak without any emotion, but his voice cracked.

"I couldn't let you leave this way."

He shook his head, his thoughts hurrying in as many directions as the airline passengers around him were.

"How'd you even find me?"

"Those secret texts between you and my brothers weren't all that secret."

"Remind me to delete them from my contact list later."

"They said you were trying to fly standby but that you finally got a seat."

C.J. shot a glance at the open door leading to the jet bridge and then turned back to her. "Look. There's nothing left for us to say."

"I think you're wrong."

"It's too late. I'm getting on an airplane."

Lily's eyes filled. "It can't be...too late. Two minutes. That's all I need. Please."

He shook his head, but when she took hold of his hand, he let her pull him away from the line.

"What can you possibly say—"

"I love you," she said to interrupt him. "I've always loved you. And I did lie. I said I left you for your sake, but I did it for myself all along.

"I was just scared. Of you. Of the staggering wave of feelings I have when I'm with you." She was speaking as fast as she could since she only had two minutes, but eventually she had to take a breath.

"—that will make a difference." He finished his comment from before.

She gripped her hands together so tightly that her fingers flashed white, and it was all C.J. could do not to reach out to her. But he couldn't rush to her rescue. Not this time.

"Wait, I—"

The loud beep and crackling sound that came over the intercom cut her off.

"Ladies and Gentlemen, general boarding for Flight 2336 with service to Boston Logan will begin momentarily. Please have your boarding pass out and ready. We will be boarding by zones."

C.J. pulled his pass from his pocket. "I can see that you went through some trouble to find me, and I realize that you need closure, but we're boarding, so…"

"So I'm not scared anymore. I'm prepared to fight for what I want."

He swallowed, his mouth suddenly dry. He couldn't let himself believe her, couldn't give those words the chance to burrow beneath his defenses. "I'm sorry. It's too late."

"It doesn't have to be," she said in a small voice.

As the first tear escaped from the corner of her eye and slid down her cheek, he stepped back. The need to wipe her tears was so powerful that he had to grip the handle of the roller bag with one hand and stuff his other in his pocket to stop himself.

More tears dampened her lashes and trailed toward her mouth. "I'm taking a chance here, too. Please, C.J., take a chance on me. Mom was right. We belong together."

Though his arms longed to reach out to her and his heart ached, he couldn't let himself give in this time. He turned away and hurried over to join the line of passengers. He couldn't look back.

He'd accused her of running. Was he doing the same thing, no matter how much justice he might find in being the one to leave this time? Would he be hurting only her, or was this a self-inflicted wound as well?

Just ten people ahead of him. Then eight. Then six. This was the right decision, wasn't it? A clean break. The good-bye they'd never had the first time. A chance to start over.

Four. Three. Two. One.

And he stopped.

He jerked the paper in his hand back just as the gate attendant reached for it.

"I need your boarding pass, sir."

He stepped aside to let the others behind him go ahead, but the attendant peeked over at him each time she scanned another passenger's paperwork.

When he was the only one left in line and another attendant was announcing final call for the flight, C.J. stepped to the desk again.

The attendant raised an eyebrow, studying him. "Sir, will you be flying with us today?"

He shook his head. "At least not on this flight."

"Do you have any checked baggage because if you do—"

He pointed to his carry-on, and she gave a relieved smile before referring him to her partner. As the woman went to work, canceling his ticket to give his seat to another passenger on standby, he couldn't hold out any longer. He had to look back. Had Lily stayed there, forcing herself to watch as each step took him further away from her? The spot where she'd spoken with him was nearly vacant as only a few stragglers hurried to their flights.

Something squeezed inside his gut. He was the one who'd said it was too late. Had she finally accepted his words and walked away? He had to go after her, find her and tell her he was wrong.

But then he caught sight of a woman sitting in a chair at the far side of the gate area. As his gaze connected with Lily's, his breath caught.

The woman he loved, the one who'd made a home inside his heart so long ago and had refused to leave no matter how hard he'd tried to expel her, was still there. And she was waiting for him.

Chapter 17

T Plus 4 Hours and 25 Minutes

LILY COULDN'T BELIEVE her eyes as C.J. strode her way instead of heading down the bridge to his flight. He stopped in front of her, an unreadable expression on his face.

"How did you know?"

She swiped at her tears. "What do you mean?"

"How did you know I wouldn't get on that plane?"

"I didn't." She'd hoped with everything inside of her, but she didn't say that. She couldn't get ahead of herself when she still didn't know what it meant that he'd stayed. As she rubbed her damp hands on her jeans, she asked, "So it's *not* too late?"

He shook his head. "Maybe not."

She sat perfectly still, afraid to let herself breathe. "Then what now?"

"This."

C.J. bent and took hold of her hand. He pulled her to her feet and immediately into his arms. As he lips came down upon hers, she lifted on her toes to meet him, pure joy welling in her heart. Her arms slid around his neck, and she smiled against his mouth.

He drew a line of kisses from her lips to her ear.

"I love you," he whispered when he paused there. "I've loved you all of my life."

She pulled back and looked in his eyes. "I love you, too. Man, I love being able to say that again."

He grinned at her. "Took you long enough."

It didn't seem possible that not quite twenty-four hours before, when they'd made love, she'd been convinced they they could never be together. Now her heart was brimming with hope.

C.J. kept kissing her in that amazing way he had of seducing her mouth and igniting her passion, and she happily went along for the ride. They were both out of breath when he pulled back and pressed his forehead to hers.

Only when applause and whistles broke out around them did she realize that they'd had an audience. Her hands covered her face, but she still couldn't stop smiling.

"Haven't any of those people ever seen a kiss before?" C.J. asked as he lowered into one of the vinyl seats behind them.

"Probably not like that."

He reached up for her hand and guided her into the seat next to him. Outside the huge windows, the plane he should have been on moved away from the gate.

"There goes my flight." He wrapped his arm around her shoulder and drew her close to his side. "I am eventually going to have to get on a plane though. I have to get back to work."

"You will." She paused to glance at her watch. "In about ninety minutes."

"What are you talking about?"

She reached into her purse and pulled out her own boarding pass. He studied it for several seconds and then glanced up at her.

"I should have wondered how you got past security without a ticket." He glanced at the boarding pass again. "Boston?"

She nodded. "There's another ticket for you, too. You just need to sign in."

"How did you swing two tickets?" When she lifted a brow, he added, "I saw how you were sweating the credit card bill at the grocery store."

She shrugged. "An early birthday present from my brothers. And my dad. For the next five years."

"But you live in L.A."

She met his gaze. "I don't have to."

The moment he seemed to get her meaning, he shook his head. "I can't ask you to move to Boston for me."

She straightened in her seat. Even after everything, were they still not on the same page here? "You're not asking. I'm *volunteering*."

"There are more acting opportunities in L.A. than—"

"I wasn't getting a whole lot of those, either."

He moved his head back and forth. "But your mom and dad—"

"Had their own marriage where they got to make their own decisions. A really smart guy once told me that."

"Marriage?"

He smiled as he asked it, and when she realized what she'd hinted at, her cheeks burned. After all of this time, she couldn't risk rushing him and scaring him away. But she couldn't lie about what she wanted, either. "Maybe. Eventually."

C.J. grinned again, but then his expression became serious. "Lily, I finally understand why you made that awful decision. I know we live on opposite coasts, but I can't ask you to give up your dream and your *home* just to follow me across the country."

"Do you want to be with me?"

He took both of her hands and stared into her eyes. "Yes. Absolutely. Yes."

"Then don't you get it?"

"Get what?"

She withdrew one hand and brushed the hair on his forehead. "You are *my home*."

He stared down at the hand still in his, and when he looked up again his eyes were wet. As she reached for his face, he shifted and stood.

"I told you the flight isn't for another ninety minutes. We have a while before we have to go to the other gate."

"That's not it."

"Then what?"

"Give me a minute, will you?"

He cleared his throat and then lowered himself onto one knee, right on the carpet in front of her chair.

She jerked and shook her head. "I didn't mean to pressure. You don't have to do this. Not yet—"

"Will you let me say this?"

She cleared her throat and nodded, her heart pounding.

"I did this once before, and you broke up with me and ran across the country, but I'm still going to take a risk and try it again."

She chuckled. "Not the best proposal I've ever heard."

He gestured with both hands for her to be quiet. "So, Lily, will you be my wife? Will you be my partner on this crazy journey?"

Tears welled in her eyes, and longing crowded her heart, but she had to ask him the question. "Are you sure it isn't too soon?"

He only chuckled at that. "Don't you think we've wasted enough time already?"

"Then yes."

"To which question?"

She smiled down at him. "Both."

He lifted up off the floor and took her in his arms again, his kiss full of hope and the promise of a lifetime together.

After a few minutes, he slid to her side and returned to his seat. "Big day, huh?"

"More than I ever planned for Thanksgiving. That's for sure."

"We should probably tell your family since they're funding this trip. Want to call them?"

Lily pulled out her phone and selected Phil's number from her contacts since he always had his phone on him.

"Hey, Phil," she said before hitting the speaker button. "I've got some news."

"You're engaged." It wasn't even a question.

She stared at the phone. "How'd you know?"

"Just a guess. Besides, Mom always knew best."

She smiled at that. "Yes, she did."

C.J. leaned over and spoke into the phone. "What do you think of that news, buddy?"

"Best thing I've heard in a long time. Welcome to the family."

Hoots and whistles from her other relatives could be heard in the background.

"You think *that* news is good. I've got even better."

"What's that?" Phil asked.

"What do you think about a Christmas wedding in Michigan?" He looked over to Lily and grinned. "And Christmas dinner."

Together, Lily and C.J. said, "We'll cook."

Also By Dana Nussio

Falling for the Cop
Strength Under Fire

Written as Dana Corbit
Finally a Mother
Safe in His Arms
Wedding Cake Wishes
His Christmas Bride
An Unexpected Match
Homecoming at Hickory Ridge
Little Miss Matchmaker
Flower Girl Bride
A Hickory Ridge Christmas
The Spirit of the Season
"A Season of Hope" in *Christmas in the Air*
On the Doorstep
"Child in a Manger" in *A Family for Christmas*
A New Life
An Honest Life
A Blessed Life

Learn more about Dana and find recipes included in *HOME TO YOU*, through her website, www.dananussio.com.

www.ingramcontent.com/pod-product-compliance
Lightning Source LLC
Chambersburg PA
CBHW020326130625
46549CB00003B/1034